Ashes and Rain

THE AHSENTHE CYCLE
BOOK 2

ALEXES RAZEVICH

ONE

A thick, gray silence smothered the world. Silence, and the smell of dirt—wet, sweet, and deep.

"Khe," Pradat said.

Soil—rich and loamy—crumbling between my fingers.

"Are you all right, Khe?"

"Fine," I said.

The chair beneath me was generously padded and probably comfortable, maybe even comforting, in a different situation. I sat with my back straight, knees together, feet dangling above the wood-planked floor. My nerves hummed and my skin itched from nervous sweat. I coughed into my fist.

"Do you need water?" Pradat adjusted her machines, small black orbs covered with spindly silver tubes that pinpointed colored lights on my body, and clearstone bowls of purple-red or clear liquids that pumped into my arms. She'd brought her tools with her from Chimbalay to Kelroosh, where I lived now with my new sisters, Azlii and Nez.

"No," I said. Better to stifle the cough and finish the treatment sooner—and hear Pradat's judgment on whether it was working or not.

It would have been easier for me to go to Pradat, but the doumanas—the females of our kind—of

Chimbalay had no love for me. I didn't blame them; I'd reduced much of their city to ashes when my sisters and I destroyed the lumani, who had been the secret rulers of our world.

I hadn't set out to destroy them; I'd wanted only to escape Simanca and her relentless pressure to push the crops to greater yield, even when she knew it was killing me. I'd wanted to find the orindles who might heal me. I'd found Pradat, but the lumani had found me, and had changed me into an abomination.

Pradat adjusted another light. I flinched at the sudden sting.

"It's a good sign that you feel something," she said. "It'll be over soon."

I had other reasons to stay away from Chimbalay. There were those there who might think what Pradat and I were trying to do was wrong. Those who would say that I'd had my rightful time—'see, count the age dots on her wrist'—and it was unnatural to try to stop the returning to the creator that all doumanas embraced during their thirty-fifth year. But it wasn't yet my time. It was only thirteen years since I'd broken free of the egg and stood on the world, first as a downy hatchling, and then as an emerged, smooth-skinned doumana. I wanted those years back. It was the most natural want there could be.

The day was growing old and the room felt chill. Pradat peered at her palm, consulting the instrument she wore strapped around her hand.

I watched her neck, but with Pradat you rarely knew what she felt unless she told you. It wasn't that she was unfeeling, not like Simanca or her cold-necked unitmates back at Lunge commune. Pradat had told me once that orindles spent years learning to keep emotions from showing on their necks. A patient could be frightened or get a wrong idea about her health because of an orindle's fleeting worry or concern. Orindles stifled their emotion spots out of courtesy to their patients—a sacrifice they made for their sisters. No orindle could be certified until she'd proven her control. I'd asked once what the trials were, but she'd pulled her lips into a thin line and refused to speak. I'd not asked her about it again.

A light-blue circle of light that focused on a spot between my eyes darkened to nearly purple. Heat on the back of my neck and base of my spine told me Pradat had lights focused there, too. I coughed again, harder and longer this time. She came around and stood in front of me.

"I'm fine," I said. The shame of that lie didn't show on my emotion spots. The lumani had changed me so no one would ever see my emotions again.

Pradat ran her hand over her smooth scalp, turned, and dialed off the machinery.

I sighed, glad it was over.

"There's a chance this worked," she said as she gently pried the tubes from my arms. "The calculations predict a probability, but I can't make promises."

I rubbed the spots where the tubes had been inserted. My throat prickled again, started to burn. I brought my hand up to my mouth, but couldn't stop coughing. It went on and on, a deep choking cough, my upper body pounding against the chair-back with each convulsion.

"Khe?" Pradat said.

Her voice sounded far away. My earholes felt on fire. A ringing in my head grew louder and louder. I couldn't breathe.

No! Not yet.

Thirty-five dots showed on my wrist. I'd known this was coming—had chosen to wear the scarlet gown of a Returning doumana last Commemoration Day, when we honored those who would leave us during the coming year. I'd thought—I'd believed—I would shoulder right up to that day before I fell.

Pradat moved quickly, laying things on the back of my neck, trying to put something in my arm, but I was coughing so hard and shook so violently that she couldn't set in the tube.

The room spun and grew dim, the walls and floors fading from my sight.

The smooth, gray silence settled over me again. The smell of loam, of Lunge commune; I welcomed it, and sank into the silence, sighing the word, "Nez."

Two

"Wake up. Get up," Pradat was saying. "Open your eyes."

It was sweet and peaceful here. I didn't want to leave.

"You want to see Nez again?" Pradat said. "Your other sisters? Larta? Azlii? Then you need to come back."

I did want to see them, be with them, live with them. I did. But it was soft here. So pleasant…

Pradat hit her fingers hard against my wrist. "Talk to me. Where is Kelroosh going next?"

"Two-ling commune," I muttered, surprised it was *that* that brought words back to me. Because it was merely factual, I supposed. Easy. "It's near planting time. The doumanas there need to order seeds and fertilizer."

I pried my eyelids open—like prying up a deeply buried stone. Pradat's face was only finger-widths away from mine. My head felt stuffed full of sand, my chest cramped by panic.

I grabbed her hand. "Did I Return to the creator? And then come back here?"

"You lost consciousness, that's all. Your day to Return is not this day."

A shaky sigh rattled through me.

"Keep talking," Pradat said. "Tell me about corentans. What are they like?"

I laughed a little under my breath. It made my head hurt but it was good to laugh, even that small bit.

"Corentans don't value work the way we set-place doumanas do, as a measure of our worth. They work hard, but think harmony of life matters more than anything." My voice grew stronger. Normal. "Azlii says all the doumanas and males of the world were like them before the lumani came and set about controlling our lives." I gently rubbed my left wrist, where my age dots were, but didn't look at them. "Now that the lumani are gone, I wonder if we'll all start thinking like corentans again."

That didn't seem likely though. We'd been set-place so long. Still, in the seemingly endless nights when I didn't sleep, I often wondered what we'd become in this new world. What I'd become, if I lived long enough to find out—if I wanted to know.

Pradat raised her eyebrow ridges. "Azlii says a lot of things." She touched my neck. "You'll be all right now. Safe journey, Khe. We'll do another treatment when Kelroosh lands near Chimbalay kler again. I'll make sure you don't pass out next time."

I put my hand over hers, keeping it on my neck.

"You could come with us," I said. "You've seen more of the world than most doumanas, but there are still parts to discover."

Pradat lowered her hand. "I have work to do in Chimbalay. Everything's different now. Without the lumani to guide our every move, it's hard sometimes to find our way. I should stay with my sister-orindles. It's where I can do the most good."

It was my achievement that the lumani were gone. Or my fault. I didn't regret what I'd done.

"Do you miss them?" I asked.

"The lumani?" Her too-large-for-her-face brown eyes widened. "No. I defied them, too. For much the same reasons you did."

But her neck showed a faint trace of the orange-yellow of confusion. Maybe she did, in some small way, long for the security of those times. She wouldn't be alone in that.

"I'll miss you," I said, and slid off the chair. It felt good to be closer to the planet, even with a wood floor under my feet.

"I'll miss you, too. But you have Azlii and Nez."

My throat warmed and I smiled at the mention of Tanez.

None of Pradat's emotion spots were lit. I tried to see with the new sight being changed by the lumani had given me—a way to perceive even the most hidden feelings—but that sight came and went as it pleased. I saw nothing now.

It wasn't just my new lumani vision that changed how I saw things. There was too much hard knowledge shoved in between the Khe who'd run from Lunge commune and the doumana now talking with Pradat for me to be the same. Sometimes I wanted to be that innocent again, to believe with all my heart in the joy of assigned work, *The Rules*, and the kindness of all doumanas toward one another.

Pradat's smile returned and her voice was light. "Could you ask your dwelling to open the door and let my helphands in? They'll carry the instruments back."

I didn't have to ask. Home had been listening and swung open the front door. The three helphands in their yellow hipwraps moved efficiently, gathering up the delicate instruments with a practiced skill that looked casual, but I knew wasn't. Helphands studied for years to be nearly invisible as they went about their work. They finished packing and carried the boxes out, leaving Pradat and me alone. I felt my neck warm at the sorrow of parting. It didn't matter that Pradat couldn't see my emotions on my neck; she felt them, I was sure of that.

-=o=-

Kelroosh rumbled, groaned, and shimmied—the buildings, soil, and surrounding wall of the mobile trading village shaking free of the land, aching for the sky. My stomach lurched as the corenta raised itself into the air and sped across the plain toward the hills surrounding the wilderness.

An entire village of structures and beings shouldn't be able to pick up and move whenever it felt like it. It should stay in one place, like a commune or kler, but all corentas skittered here and there over the plains. Sometimes, like now, they rose into the air to clear hills or mountains, on their way to pick up raw materials in one place and take them to another, or to gather finished goods to be delivered someplace else. It was a strange village I'd come to call home—this corenta, Kelroosh. But I'd come to love it the way I'd loved my commune, to love the corentans who seemed now more my sisters than maybe my commune-sisters at

Lunge had ever been.

Freed from the grip of the land, Kelroosh usually skimmed along inches above the greening fields, the ride smooth, the sensation of motion hardly there if you could stop thinking about the unnaturalness of it. Rising was a different tale—just enough shake that you couldn't ignore it, couldn't be unaware there was no solid world underneath. Wall had said Kelroosh loved to fly, loved to take sudden turns or dips, to feel the air blowing past its structures, to sneak up on flying birds or beastlets and give them a little scare. All the structures of Kelroosh had bent personalities. Kelroosh, being the sum of every structure and all who lived there, was very definitely bent.

As soon as Kelroosh steadied, Azlii asked Home to draw back the metal screen that covered a layer of clearstone in the ceiling. I kept my eyes on my hands. I didn't like to see clouds and sky or stars whizzing by, though in truth it was Kelroosh soundlessly whizzing, speeding along an arm's length above the ground, now that we'd cleared the hills. If we opened the windows, plenty of sound would come in. If we opened the windows, maybe we could smell the scent of aromatics as we passed over a field. That would be nice, but then the wind would blow things around the rooms and I supposed small flight-beasts or birds could be sucked in, and no one wanted that. The windows stayed closed.

"As fine a day for traveling as ever there was," Azlii said, tilting her head to look through the ceiling window, giving us a view of her stretched throat and the two emotion spots there lit with the pale-green of

11

contentment. "Makes me glad to be corentan, and not a set-placer."

Nez and I had been set-placers until not long ago—she from Chimbalay, and I from Lunge commune—but I knew Azlii meant no offense. Corentans just naturally thought they and their lifestyle were superior. Thought Nez and I should feel privileged to share it, too, no doubt.

"What would happen if we went outside?" I asked, partly to make conversation and partly to distract Nez, whom I knew didn't like flying. The true soil of Kelroosh was only about fingertips-to-shoulder deep. It seemed logical that if someone went outside while Kelroosh was traveling, she would fall through the soil.

"Pftt," Azlii said. "You think of the oddest things, Khe."

Nez tightened her grip on the pillow. "Why don't the structures fall through?"

Azlii regarded us thoughtfully. "I don't know. It's the way corentas are. Practically the first thing corentans learn as hatchlings is not to go outside during travel. It's one of the few strict rules we have. I've never wondered what would happen if someone did—it's inconceivable that anyone would."

I smiled at that. Corentans had few rules, but couldn't imagine breaking them. At Lunge, we'd had a whole book full of rules, yet I had broken many, as had Simanca, and I didn't think either of us regretted it.

Nez's neck showed her confusion and her curiosity. I smiled at that as well. Nez liked to know the why of things. We had that in common.

Azlii hiked up one shoulder and sent to Home, *Care*

to explain?

The sound like wind that was Home's laughter blew through the room. *Do you ask why your eyes don't fall out of your face? When a new structure is completed, it becomes part of the corenta, part of the whole. We are all different—Wall, the hatchings' place, the sales troughs, myself, Community Hall— as your arm is different from your neck or foot, but all of you is Azlii, and we are all Kelroosh, each part making the whole greater than each part is alone. You, Khe, and Nez became part of us that night.*

We didn't talk of that night often—the immediate aftermath of the destruction of the lumani. Pradat, Nez, Azlii, and I had fled across the plain while Chimbalay's energy center exploded behind us. Nez and I hardly knew each other then, and yet she'd volunteered to come fight the lumani. She'd known Larta and Azlii long enough, though, and it was those two who'd known the truth of the lumani and wanted them gone. I was only the final ingredient in their explosive brew.

We'd made it through Kelroosh's gate just as the corenta was rising from the plain, heading for Hawnya kler. It seemed a lifetime ago, but it was only most of a year. The plain was icy that night. The ice and snow of this year's Barren Season had melted now, and the sun rose higher above the horizon every day. The sharp, brown needles of wilderness sprout had begun to poke through the soil. Red-and-white striped buds were swelling on the awa trees.

Home made the little *kroot kroot* sound that meant it wanted our attention. I caught the look on Nez's face as Azlii and I looked up, waiting to hear what Home had to say. Moments like this were when she felt alien still, a stranger in Kelroosh, not a true sister. Corentans talked with the structures as if they were just another doumana. I'd come to think of the structures as friends, but Nez had never got the hang of it. She'd confided that sometimes she'd thought she heard whispers behind her, "Kler-born," as if she were less than a corentan, and it hurt her. She said I was as set-place as her, or Larta, or Pradat, but I'd managed to learn. Except that I hadn't. It had come along with my ability to push the crops—part of the same thing, I thought, but I couldn't explain any of it.

Setting down soon, Home sent.

I repeated Home's words aloud for Nez.

Azlii was out the door the minute Kelroosh settled. I hauled myself to my feet to follow her, but Nez grabbed my hand. I looked down at her, where she sat on the bright-blue pillow.

"Pradat?" she asked, meaning what was the chance of the treatment working, of my living out my natural lifespan.

I held my breath, thinking of what to say. Nez's neck glowed with the dark-gray of worry and the muddy-brown of fear. I exhaled—all the emotion that didn't show on my throat plain in the sound of my breath. "She doesn't know."

THREE

Azlii turned her head, glancing around the nearly full communiteria. "Quiet in here today."

Usually the doumanas of Kelroosh were boisterous after a landing. There was still talk, and sudden laughter, but it fell away, leaving empty spots that yearned to be filled.

"Tense." Nez's shoulders hiked up as she said the word.

"Mm," Azlii said. "But not tense enough to raise color on anyone's neck."

"Annoyed," I said, my mind partly on the unusual occurrence but mostly on this morning's treatment, the desperate hope that it would work.

The meal line wasn't long by the time we took bowls and spoons and joined the quickly moving queue. The plant-like scents of vero, the spice of morning stew, and the woody smell of bejong boiling on the cooker filled the air. I wasn't hungry, of course. I came to the communiteria at mealtimes because I liked the company—being commune-raised, *alone* was not something I ever wanted—and I still liked the scents of freshly prepared food. Odd that food smelled good to me when I didn't need to eat it—another change the lumani had made in me.

I was ahead of Azlii and Nez in the queue. Lon, the

doumana serving that morning, ladled half-a-bowlful of vero into my dish. These doumanas finally must have noticed that I rarely ate more than a spoonful. I took the bowl and went to find three open chairs together.

Azlii sat down hard in the seat beside me and clunked her bowl on the table.

"I asked for more," she said, keeping her voice quiet, "and was told there wasn't more. We always run a little low at beginning of First Warmth, but we've never been on halves." She scowled at her dish. "After morning meal, a talk with Binley will be in order. Perhaps the First of supplies has an explanation."

I stared down at my white bowl and the few scoops of dark-green vero.

"I can't eat a bite this morning," I said. "Here." I split my meal in two, pouring half into Nez's bowl, half in Azlii's.

Nez took hers with the yellow-orange of gratitude flaring quickly on her neck, then winking off. Azlii's neck showed the brown-yellow of annoyance, and it stayed.

-=o=-

Kroot kroot, Home sent, to get our attention. *Binley is coming.*

And? Azlii sent back without glancing away from what she was doing.

She looks worried, Home sent.

Azlii cleared her throat, got up from the pillow where she'd been going over some figures on a small, black textbox, and took a few steps toward the door.

16

Binley was in charge of supplies for Kelroosh. I didn't remember her ever coming to our dwelling before.

Home swung open the front door and Binley came inside. It hadn't been a stretch for Home to say she looked worried. The blue-red of anxiety was lit on most of her emotion spots, making her neck look bruised.

"Welcome," Azlii said, but her stance was anything but that—legs apart, her hands lightly fisted and resting near the top of her hipwrap.

Nez and I started to rise from the pillows where we sat, intending to leave the room, but Azlii said, "Stay."

At Lunge, all praise and condemnation were given publicly, all information shared among the commune sisters equally. Or so I'd believed until I discovered that Simanca, Lunge's leader, shared what she wanted and held back the rest. Corentans shared some things publicly and some in private. Maybe Nez and I were coming to the corentan view, since neither of us wanted, or felt the right, to hear the conversation between Azlii and Binley.

"Please," Azlii said, her eyes on Binley, her voice chill for the word. "Sit. I have some questions."

Binley didn't wait a breath. She burst into speech before she'd even settled onto the orange-red sitting-pillow.

"I'm glad you've called me here, Azlii. Things are getting serious. Something has to be done or we will be rationing more than the morning meal in ten days' time." The First of supplies wrapped her arms around her knees, hugging them toward her chest. "We're running out of food."

Azlii glared at her a moment. "And you've waited

this long to tell me?"

Binley shrugged, and I saw she was a bit afraid of Azlii. But that wasn't what had kept her from speaking out. Her silence had some other root.

"How did this happen?" Azlii asked, her voice softening. "We've never run this short before."

"We have extra mouths to feed." Binley glanced our way. "Not that you two make that much difference. Khe doesn't make any difference at all." She turned back to Azlii. "But last year we were rewarded nearly half again the number of hatchlings we usually get. And…" Three of her emotion spots lit with the brown-green of shame. Her words rushed out. "My predecessor made some mistakes."

I expected anger from Azlii. Commune doumanas would never blame a sister for anything. Not to a leader. But these doumanas were corentans, and so much was different about them.

Azlii nodded once slowly. "You didn't tell me because you didn't want to throw dirt at your sister's memory."

"Yes."

A small silence set in. Nothing showed on Azlii's neck, but everyone in the room could see that she was thinking.

"Our next stop is the spice growers' commune," she said. "No extra food for us there. And then we're scheduled for a weavers' commune. Nothing to eat there, either. But Lunge isn't far. We could detour. Trade with them for supplies."

A finger of heat raced through my chest. I hadn't been near Lunge commune since the day I crossed its borders and left my life and my sisters behind.

"Will they trade for food?" Binley asked. "It's still First Warmth. They'll have only their own storage from last year left."

"They'll have enough," I said, wondering if it was my place to speak. Lunge had the extra that I had provided for them, when Simanca had sent me, season after season, to the fields. It seemed fitting that Simanca now share that with my new sisters.

Azlii and Nez looked at me. They knew what Simanca had done—how she'd discovered my ability to make crops grow, and how she had used me even when she knew that pushing the crops was aging me. Simanca was the reason that any day could be my last, and that I would never see another Commemoration Day. Sometimes I hated her for that. Most times.

Azlii turned back to Binley. "We'll go and we'll ask. If the doumanas at Lunge won't help us, we'll try Grunewald. Someone has extra that they'll be glad to profit by."

Azlii's neck was clear, but I sensed worry in her, worry that was cool and unemotional, and so didn't show on her throat.

Binley rubbed her stomach once, then stood to go. Home swung open the front door before it was asked. Outside, a light, misty rain was falling. Binley pulled up the hood on her cloak, touched Azlii's neck, and left.

Azlii stared at the door after it closed, her bottom lip sucked in, thinking. She turned to Nez.

"I'd like you to join the trading group at the spice commune."

"Me?" The greenish-orange of amazement flickered

on Nez's throat.

"Why not? Make yourself useful."

"And do what?"

"Listen," Azlii said. "Observe. Feel."

"I'm not an empath," Nez said. "Not like Inra was."

Azlii nodded. "You are diluted, but you're the best we've got for now." She glanced at me, her eyes narrowed. "Except for Khe, of course, when she feels up to helping. Hard for a kler or commune doumana to keep a secret from her—she sees them too clearly. Still, it never hurts during trade to have two doumanas poking around, looking for the truth of things."

"I'm honored," Nez said.

Azlii scratched her knee idly. "You can help Khe with the chair, if she needs it."

I didn't like mention of the chair. It reminded me that for what I'd gained when the lumani changed me, there was much I'd lost. Some days I felt strong enough to walk on my own, and on those days I was happy to join the trading crew; it made me feel useful, a contributing sister in the corenta. If I felt weak, Nez would have to push me in the special chair that glided a hand's breadth above the ground, like a transportation vehicle, but needed a helper to steer it. Azlii had procured it somewhere—she wouldn't say how it came into her possession, just laughed when I asked and said, "If your spots could light, Khe, I would hope they would be bright with the brown-green of shame at your rude behavior. A gift is to be accepted, not questioned."

I'd kept my thoughts about that to myself. The lumani had given me gifts too.

-=o=-

Nez stared out the window and shivered. "Looks cold."

In the late afternoon, Nez, Azlii and I were warm and comfortable inside Home. I stood next to Nez, sharing view through the clearstone. The sky was grayish and the air had the shimmery look of chill. Home had a firecave set into the wall of the receiving room but we rarely used it, even through Barren Season. I fastened on a new hipwrap Azlii had given me, and asked Home, *How do you keep us so warm?*

Home chuckled low. *That's why I like you, Khe. You are not corentan, and yet are wise enough to know it is I who keeps you warm when snow is on the ground and cool when the sun batters the world. I do it with my stones, transferring heat and cold back and forth, inside to outside, so that all are comfortable, myself included.*

I'm impressed, I sent.

Rightfully so, Home sent.

Azlii handed Nez and I each an intermediary's cloak, with one brown and two green stripes running down the front. Nez tried to hide her smile, but we both saw it. She wrapped the cloak over her shoulders and seemed to grow a little taller. Intermediaries carried information from every commune and kler in their heads—who made what, what it was worth last year and the year before and the year before. To wear the cloak was an honor. Nez didn't have that information, nor did I, but we didn't need it. Azlii only wanted us to observe. She handed us thick, white neck collars as well, to hide our emotion spots during trade, though it

21

was unnecessary for me.

"Walking or riding, Khe?" Azlii asked.

I'd felt stronger since Pradat's treatment, my legs and arms not the limp grasses they'd been since the lumani had changed me. When I felt bright, I believed that the treatment was working. When I felt dark, I believed I only imagined my new strength. Time to put it to the test.

"Walking."

Nez sent me a look that was as hopeful as it was worried.

"Good," Azlii said. "That chair is annoying."

It was even colder outside than I'd expected. I pulled my cloak close around me. The doumanas we passed on the trek through Kelroosh all wore cloaks, and several had pulled the hoods up over their heads.

Good trading, Wall sent as it swung open the main gate.

Do something about this weather while we're gone, will you? Azlii sent back, joking.

Nez drew in a breath and I could guess at what she was thinking: that maybe it had been a mistake for her to stay in Kelroosh, that she should have gone back to Chimbalay—that the kler, not the corenta, was where she belonged.

Where did I belong? Not to commune, or kler, or corenta. What was I now? Not doumana or lumani, but some abomination in between.

Kelroosh had set down on the outskirts of a fallow field. Two-ling wasn't a farming commune on the scale of Lunge, and the residence structures were only a short walk away. The doumanas of Two-ling chattered among themselves as they passed us—we heading to their commune, they heading into Kelroosh to trade. The orchard trees that lay between us and the dwellings were mostly bare-limbed, but here and there the red and purple promises of new leaves and buds showed on gray wood. The air smelled of loam.

I stared through the trees and fixed my gaze on the dwellings. I'd made it to the gate under my own power; I could make it across the field.

"The guide here is Rill," Azlii said when we reached the dwellings. "She was hurt in an accident years back. Her face is scarred and she has a damaged arm. Don't stare."

As if someone had heard Azlii's words, the door swung open on one of the buildings, a smallish cube the same grayish-yellow as the soil in the fields. The door was dun-colored as well. Three doumanas walked out—cloakless, despite the cold. The doumana at the lead had one arm cut off about a hand's breath below her shoulder. Her face was scarred on the same side as the missing arm. Nez sucked in a breath. Kler doumanas didn't see this sort of thing, and certainly it wasn't something you'd see on the visionstage, but commune life was hard and I'd seen this kind of damage before.

Azlii stepped out in front and touched Rill's neck in greeting, and I caught sight of the sixteen age dots that lay on her left wrist. I clenched my teeth and tried not to, but I couldn't stop myself. I stole a glance at my own wrist. Thirty-five dots. Foolish of me to hope Pradat's treatments would make them disappear overnight.

Rill stroked Azlii's neck in return. It seemed they knew and liked each other, but it was hard to know for certain with their emotion spots covered by the thick, white collars.

"Come join us for refreshments."

Rill turned without waiting for an answer. We followed the commune doumanas into the dun-colored building.

Inside was more comfortable and colorful than I would have guessed, looking at the plainness of the outside. The receiving room had several well-stuffed chairs with high backs and low armrests. There was a long, high-backed chair that could seat four or five doumanas. The furniture was upholstered in soft, rich fabrics, each in its own color, but the colors were harmonious. A large visionstage was set in one wall. Aromatics burning in a small brazier filled the room with a subtle, spicy aroma. Nez and I had seen country doumanas when they came into Kelroosh to trade, but this was Nez's first visit to a commune. In Chimbalay, kler doumanas sometimes made fun of commune doumanas as naive and rustic. Lunge was. But if they saw Two-ling, they'd stop their silly talk.

Rill eyed one of her commune-sisters and tilted her head. The doumana scuttled off to another room and returned pushing a rolling cart with enough goblets for all of us and a pitcher of what looked like zwas, though I doubted it was, since neither side would want to be intoxicated now.

Rill poured drinks and handed them around. I took a tentative sip. The drink was delicious, light and fruity but with a surprise tart bite that came after the first taste of sweetness.

"I've said this before," Azlii said, "but it is a pity this milt squeezing won't travel."

Rill smiled. "But then it wouldn't be so special, would it? And you might not look forward with such gusto to visiting us."

"True," Azlii said. "Then I would only come for business and out of friendship, instead of business, friendship, and milt."

The room went quiet as we sipped our drink. When Azlii had drained her goblet, she held it in her lap and said, "Now, to business."

All the doumanas in the room sat up a little straighter, all but Rill.

"What's wrong?" Azlii said.

Rill swiped her hand over her scalp. "I know the first thing you'll ask is how much fertilizer we want this year."

"First Warmth," Azlii said. "You always set your order now, based on what spice or flavoring you'll be planting this year. Is there some question about that?"

Every doumana in the room looked at Rill.

She sighed. "I don't know how much to order because I don't know what we'll be growing."

Azlii turned her empty goblet in her hands and frowned. "I don't understand."

"There's no one to tell me," Rill said. "The Powers are gone. Who makes decisions now?"

Azlii, Nez, and I stared at her. Slowly the importance of what she'd said seeped in. For as long as anyone could remember, the Powers—the lumani— had decided what each growers' commune would plant. They declared what beast would be bred on the beastkeeper communes. They set the total yardage the weaver communes would make, what colors they would use. They determined where the klers would be built, what job each kler doumana would fulfill. On and on, keeping control over our world. Until I'd destroyed them. With Azlii's help, and Larta's, and Pradat's, but it was my name the doumanas of Chimbalay cursed.

Azlii blew out a breath. "Pftt. Decide for yourself. What do you want to grow this year?"

Rill folded her hands in her lap. "We could plant again what we'd planted last year, I suppose."

"Fine," Azlii said. "Then you'll want the same order that you had last year."

Rill nodded and said, "Yes. Well, maybe not."

Azlii waited for her to continue.

"We've had some calamities," Rill said. She nodded toward one of her sisters.

"It was my fault," the commune doumana said. "I would have sworn I'd shut the storage doors tight, but I must not have. Vermin got in and ate a good portion of our seed."

"So you see," Rill said, "I can't say how much we'll need because I don't know how many fields I can fill."

"I can get more seed for you," Azlii said. "It shouldn't be too much trouble to find a commune with extra they'd be willing to trade. Or some new crop, if you want to branch out."

The scars on Rill's face turned white as the blood drained from her face. "New? I wouldn't know what new to grow. How could I decide that? What if every growers' commune picked new crops based on whim?

It would be chaos."

Azlii's face stayed as smooth as clearstone. It was fortunate she wore a collar, or the colors of annoyance would be there for everyone to see. Corentans can't understand what it's like to be a commune dweller.

But I understood Rill's hesitation. It would never do for each commune to choose for itself. What if everyone decided to grow kiiku because it fetched a high price? What if no one grew awa because of how difficult it is to pollinate? Or didn't raise preslets because of their nasty dispositions, leaving us without their warm feathers to line our cloaks? There had to be balance, enough of everything.

"I know what you mean," Nez said softly into the long silence that had grown in the room. "It's very difficult to make this kind of decision. As your commune's leader, it's your responsibility to make sure your sisters thrive. If you're wrong, your commune could suffer. Your sisters could suffer."

Relief flooded across Rill's face. "Yes."

"But if you do nothing," Nez said, "your sisters will certainly suffer. You have to make a decision."

Rill stared at Nez a long moment and then said, "We'll plant what seeds we have. Nothing new. Nothing untried. Nothing that could be a mistake."

"How much fertilizer will you need for that?" Azlii asked.

Rill's eyes opened wide. "I have no idea."

Four

Azlii's steps were hard and quick crossing the distance back through Kelroosh. She didn't speak until we were inside Home with the door firmly shut.

"I swear those doumanas have been eating villisity." Azlii undid her collar and squeezed the rim in her hand. "How hard is it to make a decision?"

I rubbed my arms, though I wasn't cold. "You don't understand what it's like to be a commune or kler doumana. Nez was right in what she said. Most things have always been decided for us. We could choose our own mate during Resonance, but everything else was decreed. When the lumani were destroyed, our comfort was destroyed too. Rill doesn't want to make a mistake that might harm her sisters."

"It's true," Nez said. "For Rill, striking out with a choice of her own is likely terrifying."

Azlii's neck lit bright with the brown-yellow of annoyance.

"Give her a bit to think about it, Azlii," I said. "She'll find her decision."

"She'd best be quick about it." The corentan tossed her collar into a corner of the room—a thing I'd never seen her do before. "We have obligations, and our own, to worry about. The day after tomorrow we leave for Bethon commune, and after that we go to Lunge."

-=o=-

I sat on the edge of my cot in the hazy half-light of dawn, listening to Nez's even breathing as she slept. My left hand lay heavily in my lap, palm up, my wrist turned so that even a glance would show what I was afraid to see, but felt compelled to look at. I said a small prayer to the creator that Pradat's treatment had worked, and looked at my wrist. My heart sank. Thirty-five age dots, each one as dark and bright as they had always been. I'd hoped at least they might fade a little, a sign that I might regain my normal lifespan.

Maybe it was too soon. It was only three days ago that Pradat had come up with a new idea of how to reverse the accelerated aging that pushing the crops had caused. I could be patient. Had to be patient. What good would frustration do?

-=o=-

Nez, Azlii, and I made our way down the meandering streets of Kelroosh towards the communiteria. Commune paths and kler streets were designed to move a doumana from here to there as directly as possible. In Kelroosh, there were no straight paths, the dwellings and structures having been built wherever they and their doumana chose. We greeted each dwelling as we passed, and nodded or said good morning to the few doumanas we met on the way.

Nez drew in a great breath. "What is that glorious scent?"

Overnight, tayhosh had sprouted alongside the paths and put out its delicate blue-green flowers for all

29

to see. Even without looking, I couldn't miss the powerful, sweet aroma. I supposed tayhosh needed such a strong scent since it bloomed for only three days, which wasn't long for a plant that needed insects to pollinate it. Lucky us, getting to enjoy its sweetness. Fortunate us, too, who would get to eat tayhosh berries later, if free-roaming insects found the flowers before they faded. The true soil of Kelroosh was shallow and very little would grow in it, which made the sudden appearance of flowers a special joy.

Azlii saw where I was looking and laughed. "Still a farming doumana in your heart, aren't you?" Her voice stayed light but one emotion spot showed a trace of the blue-red of anxiety, and another the dark-lavender of curiosity. "Are we going to lose you when we get to Lunge commune?"

My stomach clenched and my neck went hot, but colorless. I still missed Lunge and my sisters there, even after what they'd done to me. I felt safest here, in Kelroosh, with Azlii and Nez—as true or truer than any sister at my former commune. Truth was, I didn't know how I would feel when Kelroosh set down outside Lunge a few days from now. Would the anger at having my life stolen flood back, or would love for those who had been my sisters crush my heart? I was glad that Simanca never let the sisters go to a corenta, calling them places of evil.

I decided I'd stay in Kelroosh. That way I would be spared seeing those I had known and loved. Those who had betrayed me for a few extra pounds of crops.

-=o=-

Five doumanas wearing cloaks of the brightest blues, reds, and yellows I'd ever seen stood waiting at the edge of a large field at Bethon commune. I was caught by the fabrics' dazzling colors. I wanted to run my fingers over the threads, to know how that vividness felt. The desire hit me hard; I'd never had that want before. Behind them we could see doumanas hand-harvesting zind, one of the few crops that bloomed in Barren Season and set seeds in First Warmth.

"We call them the Eager Weavers," Azlii said, her voice low so as not to carry. "They do everything by hand at Bethon, no machines except for harvesting a couple of the five crops they grow to make their cloth. Their guide is very proud. She'll likely give us the full walking tour, especially now that I have two fresh faces with me."

The five waiting doumanas stepped forward to greet us, spread out like flying birds with the one I picked as the commune's leader in the front. Her cloak was an exquisite blue—the color of the clearest Growing Season sky. Her skin was a light-pinkish-red, and she was shorter than her sisters, the energetic sort, I thought, who always walked ahead of others. Who probably *thought* ahead of others, too, the way that Simanca did. I hoped she was kinder than Simanca.

When the short doumana reached us, she and Azlii didn't exchange neck touches the way Azlii and Rill had. Instead Azlii shared our names with the weavers, and the weavers' leader, Fundid, shared the names of her unitmates. That done, Fundid turned and began walking quickly across the field, never looking back to see if we were keeping up, saying loudly enough for us to clearly hear, "We grow five crops here for their natural dyes. We are, of course, best known for the remarkable shade we produce using binion: Bethon Blue."

Fundid chattered on, leading us across fields, most of them fallow now, and past various outbuildings. Through an open, wide doorway we saw a team of lean doumanas with bunched muscles in their backs, legs, and arms, beating bundles of thick, hard binion stalks against sharp metal spikes set in the dirt floor. No sound came from the building but the slap, slap of the stalks against the spikes and ground. At Lunge, we would have had a song to make the work go easier, and to keep a rhythm. It seemed Fundid gave about as much thought for the doumanas in her charge as Simanca had, maybe less.

I didn't want to think about Simanca; we'd reach Lunge soon enough.

I glanced at Nez. Her eyes were as wide as full moons, watching the weavers beat the stalks into fibers. Kler doumanas had no idea where the staples and luxuries they took for granted came from, what it took to make them. I touched her neck and smiled.

"I wish I could think-talk to you," Nez whispered. "My mind is spinning."

"We'll talk in Kelroosh," I whispered back.

We came to what I guessed must be Fundid's dwelling from the way her back suddenly straightened. I blinked, surprised at the brilliant color on the walls, a blue so pure it would have lit my spots with joy— Bethon Blue. I wondered how they'd dyed the stones to get that color.

Just before we went inside, I caught sight of a doumana who stood alone near one corner. Fundid passed by her without acknowledgement. Around that corner stood another lone doumana. Fundid paid her no mind either.

Shunned. The cruelest punishment any set-place doumana could receive. I wondered what they had done to deserve such mean treatment.

The door of the Bethon Blue dwelling was as crimson as the day-ending sky. Inside, the walls were painted the pale-green of contentment, and yet the air seemed to shimmer with the gray of worry. I didn't know if I actually saw or felt it, or just imagined a color to go with the sudden tension that seized Fundid's muscles and changed the look on her face.

There was no long chair in this room. Instead the five commune doumanas and the three of us sat in a circle on wooden chairs upholstered in a thick weave as soft and comfortable as anything I'd ever felt. I couldn't help myself. I ran my fingers over the fabric and wondered if every dwelling in this commune had chairs with whisper-soft fabric dyed in this precious and expensive color, but I doubted it. If this commune was anything like Lunge, the leader and her unit lived finer than the rest of the sisters here.

They'd prepared for our visit. A tall, clear cylinder filled with thick, dark-yellow liquid sat on a table in the middle of the circle. A stack of goblets sat beside it. One of Fundid's unitmates twisted the bung open and began filling the mugs. No one spoke. Each doumana lifted her mug as she received it and sipped the drink.

It was warm and sweet at first, but had a bitter, unpleasant aftertaste.

"Binion leaf," Fundid said, answering an unasked question. "You saw them thrashing the stalks for Bethon Blue dye. We also make a yellow dye from the leaves, and a purple-red dye from the roots."

We sipped our drinks for a bit, and then Azlii asked, "The same amount of fertilizer and mulch as last year?"

The weaver's leader smiled. "Same as last year, and the year before, and the year before that."

Of course, I thought. They plant the same crops in the same number of fields, likely only rotating fields so the crops didn't deplete the soil. This visit was more courtesy than necessity. After Rill's reaction at Two-ling commune, Fundid's certainty was a relief.

"And we'll need three new threshing stakes to replace some that were damaged."

Azlii nodded, adding the orders to those she already carried in her head. "Anything else?"

Fundid leaned forward. Her eyes were flat and serious. The gray I sensed in the air seemed to grow darker.

"News from Chimbalay," she said. "Is it true the energy center blew up and several of the Powers Returned to the creator?"

"Where did you hear that?" Azlii asked calmly.

"Kelroosh isn't the only corenta plying its trade in this region," Fundid said, and shrugged. "Doumanas talk. We saw some of it on the visionstage before all the stages went dark."

My breath froze in my throat. What would Azlii say? *Oh, yes. It's true. And here's Khe. She destroyed the Powers and plunged the doumanas of Chimbalay into a near-freezing Barren Season, and now the doumanas of Two-ling commune don't know what to plant, and who knows what other consequences of her actions are still to be discovered?*

Azlii leaned back in the chair. "That sort of information is expensive."

"No doubt," Fundid said. "How expensive?"

"Very, I would think," Azlii said. "Seven new cloaks, woven here and dyed Bethon Blue."

Fundid huffed. "Since when is gossip worth that sort of price?"

"When it isn't gossip, but firsthand accounts."

The Bethon doumanas drew in their breaths as if they were one being.

"You were there?" Fundid asked.

"I was," Azlii said. Her voice was neutral, factual—as though she were about to say nothing more important than if the sun shone outside or the sky was covered in clouds.

Fundid rested her chin on her fist and considered. I didn't need to see her neck to know that she desperately wanted to hear this tale.

"All right," she said. "Trade."

I wished I could see Azlii's neck behind the collar, to know what emotions ran through her.

Azlii steepled her fingers. "The Powers were not special doumanas, as you thought; they were creatures from another world. They ruled us for generations, so long that only we corentans know the stories of the time before they came. The creatures are gone now. Every one of them. We own our world again."

"Creatures from another world," Fundid said and

laughed. Her sisters laughed with her until they realized Azlii, Nez, and I weren't sharing their emotion.

Fundid leaned forward then, her eyes narrowed, her shoulders high. "What game is this you're playing? Your lies are an insult to our history of friendship and trust."

Azlii bolted to her feet as if slapped. She glared at Fundid, then reached up and undid her collar, showing her neck. There were emotion colors there—the ocher of impatience, the brown-purple of exasperation, but not a trace of the brown-green of shame. Not even a corentan could lie and not show shame colors on her neck.

Fundid stared a long time. Her shoulders dropped back to their normal position.

"For seven cloaks, I need the whole story."

"Pftt," Azlii said, and sat again. "Eight cloaks. One in apology."

Fundid's lips pulled tight, but she nodded.

Azlii cleared her throat. "The Powers, or the lumani, as they called themselves, discovered they couldn't reproduce on our world. They were growing old, and wanted to find a way to keep their hold on us. They devised a method of mating with doumanas."

Two of the Bethon doumanas shuddered.

"Unfortunately for the lumani," Azlii said, "they picked the wrong doumana for their experiments. She destroyed them. In the process, the energy center in Chimbalay was also destroyed. It's been rebuilt now."

I laced my fingers together in my lap, and made myself listen as though this story had nothing to do with me.

Fundid still looked skeptical, but she couldn't deny the truth of Azlii's neck, which had shown only the colors of a disturbing memory as she told the story.

"How did this doumana destroy the lu… lu…"

"Lumani," Azlii said. "But that is another story. And will cost you additional."

I could tell Fundid wanted the tale, as did her unitmates, but her mind was clicking in other directions at the same time. She stared ahead at some sight that wasn't there.

Azlii leaned forward and touched Fundid's hand. "You have a question."

The touch drew Fundid back from her thoughts.

"Every year, the Powers sent us directions on what color dyes to use, how much raw cloth to weave, how many cloaks to sew. Who will tell us that now?"

Azlii clenched her hands tight in her lap. The Bethon doumanas didn't seem to notice, each with her eyebrow ridges raised now in worry. One pleated the ends of her beautiful hipwrap with her fingers.

"You could decide for yourself," Azlii said evenly.

Fundid blinked. She sat quietly for a long moment—so long that her unitmates fidgeted in their seats, settling and resettling. Nez and I followed Azlii's lead, sitting as still as trees.

Slowly Fundid stood and undid her collar. The orange yellow of confusion showed on nearly all of her spots. She looked at one of her unitmates.

"My Second will bring the cloaks. We are done here."

"There's more to the story," Azlii said, clearly surprised at this turn of the conversation. "Sit, and I will tell you."

Fundid shook her head. "I'd hoped you would tell me the rumors were false."

She turned and walked out the door of her own dwelling as if she had found herself in a strange land and was lost.

-=o=-

The shunned doumanas still stood at their lonely corners outside Fundid's dwelling. I could see Nez was trying not to stare, but she couldn't stop herself.

"What do you think they did?" she asked, her voice low.

I shrugged. My mind was crowded with angry thoughts. I pushed the strap of the carrying bag filled with two of the lovely cloaks higher onto my shoulder. Azlii and Nez carried three cloaks each, in similar bags.

We took a more direct route back across Bethon, crossing a fallow field of rich, dark loam. I angled Azlii off until we were away from Nez.

"I'm glad Fundid didn't want to hear more of the story," I said. "In the future, if you want to tell your part in what happened in Chimbalay, do it, but not in front of me. I don't need reminding of what happened."

Azlii startled out of her own thoughts. "Did you see Fundid's neck after I suggested she decide what her commune would do? We're in for trouble, Khe, and I don't have the first idea how to stop it."

She sped her step, leaving Nez and me behind. A slight rain began to fall.

FIVE

Wall left the gate open behind Azlii, waiting for Nez and me to follow through. The misting had turned into true rain, with drops as soft as hatchling down dusting our skins. I leaned on Nez's arm. She walked slowly, but made it seem like it was the pace she wanted, rather than the only speed I could manage.

"You're angry at Azlii," she said as Wall shut the gate behind us. "I can feel it through your skin."

"Turn of phrase?"

"No," she said. "I don't know why, but I can feel your emotions. Sometimes, back in Chimbalay, I could feel Mees and some of the hatchlings, but not all of them. I never told anyone."

"But you're telling me."

She shrugged. "There's no one on this planet more strange than you, Khe. I trust you to keep my secret."

Strange was an interesting choice of words. Interesting, too, that she thought she could tell me because as different as she might be, I was more so—and therefore safe.

We trundled slowly toward the central commons, our hoods drawn up to protect our scalps from the falling rain. In the distance I could see a small group of corentans gathered in commons, their cloaks thrown off, their faces turned to the sky. I *was* different—and had sharper eyesight than any doumana should. Another gift from the lumani.

"What's it like," I asked Nez, "to feel a doumana's emotions?"

She shrugged again. "I can't describe it. It's knowing someone's true passion, in their depths. We see our sisters' spots light, and we think we know what they're feeling, but we don't. We only imagine that they feel what we do when that emotion arises, that we're the same. But we're not. I never would have known the difference without *feeling*."

"Maybe you are an empath after all," I said. "It would make Inra proud if you were."

Nez sniffed, and I didn't have to be an empath or see her spots to know that thinking of her kler-sister, destroyed by the lumani, made her sad.

"Perhaps I'm her legacy," she said.

My heart closed like a fist, resenting the idea. I couldn't say why but, in my depths, if Nez were to be anyone's legacy, I wanted her to be mine.

We were close enough to the commons now that Nez, too, could see the rain-loving doumanas. More had joined them while we walked. Azlii, who'd already reached them, waved to us and rushed back, the crimson of joy lit on her spots, all thought of Fundid and any coming troubles evidently banished from her mind.

"Early rain is lucky," she said, holding out her arms as if to embrace us. "It'll bring lush crops, and everyone will have enough to eat. We're celebrating. Come join in."

"Does rain turn them into babblers?" Nez asked,

but smiled.

The corentans could have been mistaken for babblers easily enough. Some still had their faces upturned to the sky, thin rivulets of water sluicing down their cheeks. Others were hopping up and down, and still others swaying with their arms in the air, like trees in a wind. Azlii had set her carry-sack down on a flat rock on the Commons edge.

"Come on," she said. "I'll teach you both to dance."

Nez pulled up her shoulders. "Khe is tired."

"Pftt," Azlii said. "You set-place doumanas have no idea how to enjoy yourselves." She turned and headed back toward her sisters, swinging her hips in rhythm to a song only she heard.

Nez took my elbow and started toward Home, but her eyes lingered on the others and a faint blue-yellow blush of wanting was on her neck.

"Let's stay," I said. "I'll sit and watch. You dance."

"Are you sure?"

I nodded. Nez grinned and trotted off after Azlii.

I folded my legs under me and sat on the damp ground, my carry-sack and Nez's balanced on my lap. The cold seemed to crawl into my bones. I rearranged my cloak so it was under me, which was better. I'd never seen anyone dance outside of Resonance, and then only the males, trying to attract our attention so we'd choose them for mating the one free choice we could make in our lives. I slipped my fingers into one of the sacks and stroked the feather-soft fabric of a Bethon cloak, for the comfort it brought.

-=o=-

Kroot. Kroot kroot, Home sent, and sounded very excited. Azlii, Nez, and I were in the receiving room. Azlii and I looked up expectantly.

Wall has spotted something, Home sent.

Kelroosh was in flight, traveling toward Lunge commune. I wondered what Wall could have seen— something in the air, or something below us? I was halfway to my feet to climb the stairs to the upper story and try to see when Home sent, *Hatchlings! Wall says there are hatchlings on the plain.*

"That doesn't make sense," Azlii said aloud.

Nez looked up from the cloth she was decorating with colored threads sewn into patterns. "What?"

"Home says that Wall has spotted hatchlings on the plain below us," I said.

"It's past gathering time," Nez said, her hand held paused in mid-stitch. "Why would they be on the plain?"

Azlii pressed her lips together and thought-talked to Kelroosh, *Something's wrong. Please set down as close to them as possible.*

Of course something's wrong, Home sent. *We're already slowing and looking for a spot to land.*

My stomach lurched as Kelroosh came to a sudden stop. Nez swayed forward on her pillow and yelped, her cloth, needle, and thread flying from her grasp. She braced her hands against the floor. Azlii must have been used to this kind of thing because although she swayed on her pillow, she rode out the stuttering stop as if it were merely an inconvenience. We landed with a bang that shuddered through my body, from my feet, up my spine, to my skull.

Nez blew out a loud breath of air, clearly glad to have lived through the experience. Azlii got to her feet quickly, grabbed her cloak from the wall peg and headed for the front door, which Home had already opened. She threw a glance over her shoulder.

"Come on," she said. "You two are the hatchling experts, not me."

Nez and I took our cloaks from the pegs and followed after her.

Dust swirled in the air, spewed up from our sudden landing, and was caught in the mist that fell from the grey-brown sky. Corentans spilled out of their dwellings, chattering with each other, and heading toward the main gate.

The gate was closed when we reached it. Wall sent, *Azlii is in charge. I'll open the gate when she says so.*

I realized that Wall had only told Home, and Home had only told us about the hatchlings on the plain— which explained why the rest of the corentans had necks aflame with the blue-red of anxiety.

Azlii held up her hand and pitched her voice so everyone could hear.

"Wall has spotted some hatchlings alone on the plain. I don't know why they're there. Confusion with the pick-up orders or something. Khe, Nez, and I will go speak with them and see what we can learn."

The other corentans had gone quiet, listening to Azlii. Now they burst into words, like calling birds at sunrise.

Wall, Azlii sent, *if you would, please.*

The gate opened. Nez and I followed Azlii out onto a flat, wild plain. New sprouts of denish and tano poked here and there through the soil. The dirt was rusty brown-red. A copse of trees, their leaves beginning to bud in the same shade as the soil, stood before us. Through the trees we could see a small group of downy, yellow hatchlings huddled together. They stared at us with large, frightened eyes. Thanks to the lumani's tinkering that made my ears as sharp as my eyes, I heard their soft mewling even at this distance.

Or maybe it wasn't the lumani's doing. I could tell Azlii didn't hear it, but Nez had her head cocked, her left ear hole turned slightly toward the sound. Azlii liked hatchlings—everyone did—but Nez and I treasured them in our hearts. Maybe that made us more attuned.

"They're crying," I said, and Nez nodded.

Azlii looked at us. "What are they doing here? They should have been picked up and distributed already."

"They must be hungry," Nez said. "They will have licked their eggs dry by now."

Seeing us, the hatchlings clustered closer to one another—if that was possible—and kept their wary eyes on us. Nez smiled and started towards them, making soft, cooing noises in her throat. The hatchlings watched her come, some shifting foot to foot, but they didn't run away. Maybe they were too weak to run. They were very thin.

When Nez was about halfway to them, she turned back and waved for us to come. Azlii stayed where she was, but I headed toward the hatchlings, cooing much as Nez had. I walked as fast as I could manage, but didn't rush, so I wouldn't scare anyone.

"Who is the bravest among you?" I said when I reached them.

A few looked at the ground, but most turned their heads and looked at one particular hatchling. It stood tall and smiled tentatively at Nez and me. It didn't have emotion spots yet. Those wouldn't emerge until it did, leaving its hatchling state behind and becoming a doumana.

Or a male, I thought suddenly. Hatchlings all look similar, not getting their own true faces and bodies until after emergence. This group could be all female, all male, or a mix of both. We had no way of knowing without a closer look. But they were alone and starving; what sex they were was of no matter.

I looked at the bold hatchling. "What's your name?"

"Darnan." Its voice was soft and weak.

"What are you doing here? Are there more of you?" The nesting ground was large. There would have been many eggs laid here. There should be more than the twice-four hatchlings standing before us.

"Only us," Darnan said. "A big thing that moved along the ground came. Doumanas were in it. They grab up everybody until the box was full. They left us behind."

Nez knelt next to me. Her spots were lit brown-black in anger.

"How could the gatherers leave them?" she whispered.

I didn't have an answer, only the guess that the gatherers meant to return, but something had happened.

Another hatchling spoke up, drawing me back from

my thoughts. "We had eats, but they're gone."

Azlii strode up beside Nez and me, and spoke low. "We'll take them with us. This place isn't a corentan mating ground, so they can't stay with us long, but we'll reason out a solution. We'll have to find someone who knows how to tell doumana from male hatchling."

"I can do that," I said. I'd never seen a male hatchling, but I'd seen plenty of proto-doumanas and thought I could figure out if there was some sort of marking distinction.

"My work in Chimbalay was at a hatchling house," Nez said. "I know the differences."

"Maybe we should separate them now, then," Azlii said.

Nez's spots flared brown-black again. "You can't leave any of them here. They won't survive."

"Pftt," Azlii said, but no spots lit on her neck. Whatever she felt wasn't strong enough to note, or to stop our taking all the hatchlings.

Nez pointed to Kelroosh and said, "That is our living place. It'll be yours too, for a while. Come on now and we'll find you something good to eat."

Even the shyest hatchling grew excited at the thought of food—and likely shelter and company, too. They gathered around us like a soft yellow cloud, and together we returned to Kelroosh.

The rest of the corentans were gathered by the gate. Wall was quick to take credit for having spotted the hatchlings, sending how fortunate it was that it had superior senses, seeing and hearing far more than mere doumanas could imagine. Wall did have excellent hearing, and had sent the gist of our conversations with the hatchlings to the doumanas who'd stayed behind. Most were excited to have the hatchlings among us, but I heard more than one corentan complain that they were just more mouths to feed.

-=o=-

"They're right," Azlii said once we'd settled the newcomers in with Kelroosh's own young, leaving Nez at the hatchling house to help with the transition. "It is more mouths to feed, and we all know how hatchlings can eat." She looked at me. "Is Simanca vain?"

I half laughed under my breath—at the abrupt change of subject and at the question. "She has her vanities. Mostly about what a brilliant leader she is for Lunge. Why?"

"Does she like to decorate herself? We have those Bethon Blue cloaks. Very difficult for a commune leader to ever have enough credits to buy one of those. Do you think she would lust for one enough to trade for the food we need?"

The cloaks were beautiful, tightly woven and as soft as feathers. A cold part of me didn't want Simanca to have anything so fine.

"She'd lust more for the hatchlings, unless she's completely changed who she is in her heart."

Azlii raised her eyebrow ridges. "Good. Two solutions in one transaction. We'll head for Lunge tomorrow at first light. In the meantime, I hope Nez can figure out which of those hatchlings are doumana, and which not. Simanca likely wouldn't be too happy if we left her with males."

-=o=-

47

Azlii and Nez were quiet as we sat at the table, eating the morning meal in Home instead of at the communiteria today. Not that it was all that unusual for Nez to be quiet, but Azlii was normally a wellspring of words. She reminded me of my sister at Lunge, Thedra, that way. I was quiet myself. My heart ached with wanting to see Thedra today, and Jit and Stoss, my unitmates at Lunge, the place that had been my home until just a few seasons ago. That life seemed a fever dream now, and all that had happened these last few seasons my only real life. But Lunge was real. Simanca was real. The ache in my heart turned to nerves and resentment.

Kelroosh had settled onto the plain outside Lunge commune the night before. Soon Wall would throw open the front gate and Simanca and her unitmates would come to trade.

I huffed out a harsh breath.

"Thinking of Simanca?" Azlii said, not looking up.

I nodded and looked down at my bowl. I'd eaten none of it, and thought I should donate it for the hatchlings.

Corentans usually shared a communal morning meal—a daily reminder that all in Kelroosh were one—but ate alone at night, for individual reflection and contemplation. Of all the doumanas of Kelroosh, only Azlii shared her home, and that was only out of kindness to Nez and me, kler and commune doumanas that we were, who couldn't imagine living without our sisters always near. Each night they set a place for me, and served a meal, as if somehow my appetite would return and we could all go back to who and what we were before the lumani.

"You don't have to meet with Simanca," Azlii said. "But you should."

"Why should she?" Nez asked. "Khe doesn't miss Simanca. There's no love between them. Simanca isn't going to suddenly break down and apologize for her ill treatment of Khe—not from what I've heard about her."

Sweet Nez; the one doumana I told most everything to. I didn't know why her and not Azlii. Ever since we'd come to Kelroosh, I'd felt more in harmony with Nez, maybe because we were both set-placers.

"Because," Azlii said, "the unfinished past haunts her. Better to seize the moment and see Simanca for what she is, not what Khe has built her up to be."

"I want to seize her by the throat and strike her down," I said, a little ashamed of my feelings, a little embarrassed by my own honest outburst. But speech was all I had left, now that my spots no longer lit—the only way for my sisters to know my emotions. Except Nez. She knew already.

"Weast is the only other being who made me feel this way." I hadn't said that name since leaving Chimbalay the night we'd destroyed the all the lumani, including Weast—the one that had chosen me to be its mate. The one that had made me what I now was. Weast and Simanca. Funny how I thought of them together.

"My point exactly," Azlii said. "See her. Strike her if you want to."

I laughed without humor. "I thought corentans were against violence."

"Mostly," Azlii said.

"I'll meet with her." I was amazed at the words that had jumped from my mouth. Only seconds earlier I never would have said them.

Opening the gate, I heard Wall sending to the doumanas of Kelroosh, alerting them to be ready.

"How are you feeling today?" Azlii asked. Meaning, was I strong enough physically to see Simanca?

"Good," I said. "Better than the day of the dancing doumanas. I was tired then."

Pradat's treatment seemed to be holding—or more rightly, coming and going. My body wasn't as strong as it had been, but was stronger now than after Weast had finished changing me. Maybe it wasn't too late. I held on to the hope for a moment, and then threw it away. Too early to hope when disappointment could be so close on its heels. Commemoration Day was coming, if I made it that far.

"Your Simanca likes to meet in Community Hall." Red-purple flared on Azlii's neck, and I wondered what she thought was funny.

"Hall can't stand her," she said. "Thinks she's a beast. Always has, even before we knew you, Khe. I don't like her either. I try to get the best end of any dealings with her."

I stared, stunned. All of my life at Lunge, I'd watched Simanca visit corentas to trade for goods. She always went with only her unitmates, to spare the rest of us from contact with the evil corentans—who were only slightly less dangerous than babblers, in Simanca's telling. I'd never considered that Kelroosh might have had Lunge commune on its route, or that Azlii and the others might know the doumana who had used me so badly. *Your* Simanca, Azlii called her. *My* Simanca.

Azlii patted my shoulder. "You're going to be my best tool today. Once Simanca sets her eyes on you, she'll be too shocked to do anything but give us what we want."

The ice-blue of pleasure-in-another's-woes glowed faintly on her neck. It startled me. This wasn't an emotion doumanas allowed themselves often. We didn't have a compact word for it, and I'd only seen the color a few times, most often on Simanca. As nervous as I was about seeing Simanca again, a part of me shared Azlii's dark glee at the idea of breaking Simanca's perfect composure. I saw it in my mind's eye—Simanca, always sure of herself, always calm, shocked and weakened by the sight of me. The thought cheered me. Some.

"What I'd like you to do," Azlii said, fastening a collar around her neck, "is wait outside Hall until I call for you. Hall can keep you informed about what's going on inside. I'd tell you myself, but if I have to think-talk to you, it splits my concentration."

I nodded agreement and let out a sigh. The sigh helped, but my heart kept pounding in my chest. My neck felt hot. I didn't like that Simanca still had power over me. I breathed in, slowly and deeply.

Azlii and Nez put on light cloaks for the short walk to Hall. I put on a heavier one, not knowing how long I'd be waiting outside. The weather had turned cold for First Warmth, and the mist, drizzle, and occasional hard rain had hardly let up for days. Even the corentans who'd danced in the first drops were beginning to grumble.

Hall kept up a running commentary on the conversation inside it, not only telling me what was said, but how each doumana behaved, who leaned forward, who leaned away, whose eyes narrowed during the negotiations.

Hall laughed with that deep wind sound and sent, *Doumanas cover their necks to hide their emotions, but their bodies still speak.*

We don't notice that, I sent back. I swung my arms to warm myself. The effort was tiring. I leaned against Hall's side for support.

Doumanas should pay attention, Hall sent. *But you do. You pay attention without knowing you've paid attention. I see it in the way your body moves—you tilt your head very slightly and go still. You must begin to notice these things in yourself if you are to be the most you of all.*

Before I could reply, Hall sent. *Azlii wants you now.*

I took a step, half stumbled, and clenched my fists in frustration. This was no time for my legs to go weak. It wasn't only physical weakness that made my legs feel like water reeds—fear stripped the strength from my muscles.

Tav would be with Simanca, I told myself. Sweet Tav, who had schooled me as a hatchling, and had always been kind.

Hall swung open the door and I walked into the main chamber. Azlii was already looking my way. I watched as the doumanas of Lunge shifted their eyes to see what she was looking at. I focused on Simanca. Her mouth dropped open, and then snapped shut. She pulled herself up as tall as she could. Her body was as

52

stiff as an icicle, her face a mask of one pleasantly surprised.

"The creator is kind," she called, clapping both palms against her thighs. "You're alive, Khe. And well."

Tav jumped up from her chair and ran across the room, stopping in front of me. She stroked my neck and muttered, "I knew. I knew it all along."

I stroked her neck in return, truly happy to see her.

Simanca still wore a pretended joy on her face, but her eyes were as hard and cold as dead wood. She kept her gaze on me, muttering so low that only I, with better hearing, heard her. "This changes things."

Her smile turned true, but it wasn't from happiness at seeing me. "Is this where you've been all this time, Khe—in the corenta?"

"Trying to come back to us," Tav said and stroked my neck again. "All this time, trying to return to Lunge commune however she could."

I didn't have the heart to correct her.

"Now that we've found each other again," Simanca said to Azlii, "of course Khe will be returning to Lunge. We thank you for bringing her to us." She swiveled her head back to me. "Your sisters miss you very much. They feared you were returned to the creator. They will be delighted to have you back in your rightful place."

My mouth felt dry. "This is my place, and these my sisters." I spread my arm to encompass Azlii, Nez, and the whole of Kelroosh. Even as I said it, I thought of Jit, Stoss, and Thedra, and knew they, too, were my sisters, that the bond with the doumanas of Lunge would never be broken. That like Nez, I was of two places, and of neither.

Tav stared at me as if I had shunned her. Which I suppose I had.

Simanca rested her hands on her lap and smiled. "Azlii, shall we talk trade? Thanks to Khe, we have a good store. What would you like, how much, and what do you offer in return?"

"What would *you* like?" Azlii said. "We visit almost every type of commune and kler. I can take your order now and deliver to you later."

Simanca laced her fingers together, never raising her hands from her lap. Silence spread in the room like a shadow.

This wasn't going the way Azlii had expected—I could see that. I didn't know what she had expected: that upon seeing me, Simanca would fall to her knees, confess her sins and, in atonement, beg to give Kelroosh all the supplies they needed? Azlii should have listened more closely when I talked about my old commune leader and what had happened in the fields at Lunge.

What do you think, Hall? I sent, but Hall chose this moment to stay silent.

I could feel my strength slipping, almost as if Simanca were pulling it out of me and into her.

Strike while the enemy feels strong, Hall sent suddenly.

Azlii said, "As you know, Kelroosh also has an almost unique access to special types of information. Perhaps there is something you'd like to know?"

Simanca likely felt hidden and safe behind her collar, but I saw how greed bubble in her heart and spread over her skin like a coat of thick brown mud.

Lumani sight—it revealed not only the emotions that might show on a doumana's neck, but every deep and hidden feeling as well. I sent a quick thought-talk to Azlii: *You have her attention now.*

"We've recently come from Chimbalay," Azlii said. "The First of the guardians, a doumana called Larta, is like a sister to me. She tells me things…"

I shifted my gaze to Azlii. She must feel desperate to offer up her connection to Larta. Which meant the food hoards were more depleted than she'd let on.

Simanca lifted one shoulder as if this precious offer were of no matter to her. "I only want what is rightfully Lunge commune's. Khe will return to us. We will give you the food you need."

"I won't go," I said.

Tav, Gintok, and Min stared at me, their eyes wide. The old Khe, the Khe they knew, would never have spoken so boldly.

"It's not your decision to make," Simanca said softly, her confidence as plain as the rain running down the outside of the windows. "As the leader of Lunge commune, and with Azlii, as the leader of this corenta, it is our place to decide."

Azlii snickered under her breath. "You don't understand corentans, do you? We have no leaders with final authority, only guides. Khe will make her own choice."

My lumani eyes were still working. Behind her collar, I saw the brown-black of anger began to rise on Simanca's neck, and fade as she saw a new way to win.

"Let Khe decide then. My offer is that Lunge will provide you with the goods you've asked for, providing that Khe returns to us. If she doesn't return, sadly we would be unable to help you."

My skin felt hot. Nez drew in a sharp breath, but Azlii merely shrugged.

"There are many farming communes," she said.

But none with the extra supplies Lunge has, I sent to her. *I know*, Azlii sent back. *Don't base your choice on that.*

I made my voice sound with a calmness I didn't feel. "We'll be here a few days. I'll think about it."

"Do that," Simanca said. "I will tell your unitmates we've found you again, in the corenta. They'll want to see you."

Simanca always knew my weaknesses.

"Please join us at Lunge tomorrow," she said to all three of us now, "for a celebration of the new season."

I was not, absolutely not, going to step foot onto Lunge commune. It would break my heart, one way or another.

Azlii bent her lips in a returning smile. "Thank you. We joyfully accept your hospitality. Unfortunately Khe has been ill and won't be able to come."

Simanca's smile faded. "I'm sorry to hear that."

"Perhaps Jit, Stoss and Thedra could come here, to Kelroosh?" I said. "You said they would want to see me. It would be sad for them to miss this chance, in case I decide not to return to Lunge."

Let her wriggle free of that.

She sniffed. "What a wonderful suggestion. Should they come this evening, or are you too weak and would prefer to wait?"

"This evening would be fine," I said, though I knew it was probably a very bad idea.

Six

When Nez and I first came to live with Azlii, Home had added on a second story sleep-quarters for us. It was quite proud to be the only structure in Kelroosh with a room on top. I stood at the west-facing window on the top floor, my heart beating fast, watching my commune-sisters while they were much too far away to see me. They stood at the open gate of Kelroosh, in the gray air of just-beyond-sunset, hesitating. Stoss, the most timid, was likely ready to turn and run. I hoped she wouldn't. All their lives, all of mine in Lunge, we were told that corentas were evil places filled with cruel doumanas. My sisters had to be wondering what horror was about to crush them.

I pulled on a dry pair of foot casings and a light cloak, and went outside to greet them.

My neck burned like a sun inside my skin as I approached my commune unitmates. My heart felt squeezed. I'd missed them—that was the truth of it. I couldn't see my once-sisters' necks. Simanca had swaddled them in thick white collars, as if they had come to trade.

Maybe they had. Maybe Simanca had only let them visit so they might convince me to return to Lunge. Maybe Simanca had made them come, her words about how they missed me lies. I wanted to see them with lumani vision—as true, or truer, than seeing the spots that bloomed on their necks. All I saw now was a dim blue-red of nervousness, and that could have come from anything. It was the color my commune-sisters would have seen on my own neck if anything had shown there.

They must have worked up their courage, because they came through the gate and walked slowly toward the commons, their heads turning this way and that, taking in the strange sights. Even Thedra seemed agog, which made me smile inside; Thedra, always so sure of herself, never in doubt or thrown off her feet.

"Jit!" I called. "Stoss! Thedra!"

I walked as fast as I could toward them, meeting them in the commons where I'd watched my corenta-sisters dance. It took all my energy to keep going and I was panting hard and stumbling by the time I reached them. Jit steadied me—her arms stiff and unsure.

We huddled in a small clump on the commons, looking at each other. Community Hall stood on one side of the open space, and was no doubt curious about the visitors, but kept its thoughts and questions private. I straightened myself and took a small step back from Jit. We stood in awkward silence, scanning from face to face. Likely they didn't know what to say any more than I did.

I wanted to know what they felt. "You don't need to wear those collars. Not in front of me."

"Simanca said—" Stoss began.

"It's Khe," Thedra said, cutting her off. "Do you think she's going to eat us up and have kiiku squares for aftermeal treat?"

She reached up and pulled off her collar with a quick finger jerk. I almost laughed. The color on her throat was the bruised brown-purple of exasperation— at her sister's strict adherence to the rule Simanca had set down, I guessed. I never knew why Thedra got away with her small rebellions. I think I never loved her so much as in that moment.

Jit reached up and undid her collar, her eyes locked on my face. Her neck was crimson with joy.

Stoss slowly undid her collar, but held it in front of her chest like a shield. On her I saw the orange-yellow of confusion and the purple-gray of concern.

Jit's gaze slid from my face down to my throat. The spots on her neck changed from crimson to dark-brown. "No colors for us, Khe? You feel nothing at seeing us?"

Heat spread through me, prickling my skin.

"It's a long story," I said. "Believe me, I couldn't be happier to see you three, my unitmates and sisters. I feared I never would again."

"Let's not hear your long story standing out in the open," Thedra said, setting one hand on her hip in that way she had. "Don't you have a dwelling or some place we could go?"

I half-laughed, embarrassed. "Yes, of course; this way."

They followed me down the meandering paths, tayhosh blooming at our feet, filling the air with its fragrance. I talked as we walked. "This is our community hall. Kelroosh also has this large commons area right beside it where the sisters come to mingle."

My commune-sisters gasped at the corentan

dwellings, each one as individual in size, shape, and color as the doumana who lived within. "The dwellings all look different because each doumana makes it look the way she likes. Corentans mostly live one to a dwelling, not like commune doumanas, living with their unit. I don't live alone though, and I wouldn't want to. I live with two others—Azlii, a corentan, and Nez, from Chimbalay."

They eyed the trading stalls, empty now, but which at other times were loaded with goods and crowded with kler or commune doumanas looking to fill their carry-sacks with supplies from all over Region One.

"Most communes let every sister come to Kelroosh to trade for what they want," I said.

Their necks changed colors so quickly it was hard to keep track of what they were feeling: curiosity, anxiety, surprise, amazement. I understood how they felt. The world was so much bigger and varied than my old commune-sisters could imagine. It pleased me to show them this tiny slice of what lay beyond Lunge.

When we reached Home, Stoss let out a little yelp and jumped back when the door swung open as we approached.

Thedra's neck clouded brown-yellow with annoyance. "Is this corentan humor, Khe? Hiding behind a door to make it seem it opened itself? Are your unitmates inside, laughing at us?"

Stoss muttered, "Simanca was right. Corentans are evil."

I saw then that what I'd been telling them had made them uncomfortable. Too much was new, too much was strange. The idea that Home opened the door itself might be more than they could take in. "Things are a little different here." I smiled. "Come inside. We have so much to talk about."

I touched my hand to the outside jamb and sent Home a message: *These are my sisters from Lunge. We would appreciate some privacy. And no tricks, please.*

Home grumbled, but I trusted it would politely turn deaf while Jit, Stoss, and Thedra were inside, and do nothing to announce its sentient presence.

We settled onto the pillows in the receiving room. Maybe it was their shock at how strange to them things were in Kelroosh, but their voices seemed to have dried up like old wells. My own brain felt suddenly damaged, unable to think of what to say either. We sat in uncomfortable silence, my sisters' glances roving over the walls, ceiling, table—anything to not look at me, or each other. I expected it would be bold Thedra who would end the silence, but it was Jit, twisting the first two fingers of her left hand in the hold of her right.

"Why did you leave us, Khe? What had we done to make you despise your sisters?" She stopped twisting her fingers. "Simanca put it around that you'd turned into a babbler, but she had to swallow that back to ask us to come here today. You aren't insane, so it must be that you shunned us. I want to know why."

I held out my left arm, turning it wrist up. They'd seen my thirty-five dots before. Still Jit drew in her breath.

"You know that pushing the crops to grow bigger and faster at Lunge was aging me. When the thirty-fifth—the last—age dot appeared on my wrist, I decided I wanted to make my own choices about how to live the time left to me. I wanted to be a doumana, not a machine run nonstop until it broke beyond repair." I swallowed hard. "Mostly I hoped to find someone who could fix me. I went to Chimbalay, to find the orindles. If anyone could stop my aging, it would be them."

My sisters stared at my mouth while I spoke—I supposed because there were no spots on my neck to tell them my emotions. Without that, there were only words left.

"Weren't you afraid?" Stoss said.

"Very."

Jit's voice rushed like storm water down a hillside. "Our purpose is to serve our community. Lunge commune nurtured you, loved you, and you left us as though we were of no more importance than dead stalks in a field." Two emotion spots lit brown-black with anger.

I reached out to touch her neck.

She brushed my hand away. "We were a unit. *The Rules of a Good Life* say a unit is many bodies, but one head and heart. You took part of us away. You hurt us."

My view flickered back and forth between my commune-sisters. Stoss's neck was nearly all blue-red with anxiety—for Jit's sake, I thought, not for mine.

This is what the lumani had made us—creatures so compliant, so attuned to *The Rules*, that my commune-sisters blamed me for choosing myself over the unit. Maybe I blamed myself a little as well.

After what seemed too long a pause but probably was only seconds, Jit pulled herself up, trembling. She rocked back and forth on the balls of her feet. "I'm sorry we came to see you. It was better when we thought you'd turned babbler and returned to the creator. I'm going back to Lunge now. Simanca can shun me. I don't care."

Then I saw. Simanca had sent my unitmates to convince me to return with them. She'd counted on my affection for them, but failed to reckon with Jit's grief and anger.

Thedra and Stoss remained seated. Jit's gaze bounced wildly back and forth between them. She wouldn't look at me.

One ocher spot, the color of impatience, lit on Thedra's neck. "Sit down, Jit. You know what else *The Rules* say? 'Walk not in anger, for that path is full of stones.' Stay. Listen to Khe."

Slowly, Jit lowered herself back down to the floor pillow.

"I never meant to hurt you," I said. "No more than you likely meant to hurt me when you saw what pushing the crops was doing and never thought to protest."

"We did, though," Thedra said. "Protest. To Simanca. Jit most of all. Of course it was useless."

"We begged her to leave you be," Stoss said. "We said that you'd Return too soon. That it was unnatural. That we didn't want the extras that pushing the crops gave to Lunge. Nothing mattered to Simanca except getting more hatchlings, and then winning the Ten-Year Competition. We fought hard, Khe. We did."

I tried to respond, but couldn't make the words come out. All those lonely days and nights when I'd thought my sisters cared more for the extras my talent brought than they did for me—I'd been wrong.

They could have tried harder.

"Why didn't you tell me?" I finally managed to say. "It would have meant much."

Jit and Stoss looked at their feet.

"Simanca," Thedra said. "She said if we told you we'd spoken to her, we'd be shunned—and that might not be the worst of it. We were scared. *The Rules* say, 'Honor your leader and obey.' We did—and failed you."

Jit and Stoss kept their heads down, but Thedra held her head up and stretched her neck, awash in the brown-green of shame—as if the act of boldly displaying this color was part of her atonement.

I reached over and stroked her throat. Jit and Stoss must have caught the flash of movement because they both looked up. I stood and walked over to stand in front of Jit. I squatted on my heels and stroked her neck. I did the same with Stoss. Jit kept her hands folded in her lap, ashamed. Stoss reached up and tentatively touched my neck in return.

"You were my sisters, my unitmates, in Lunge," I said. "That bond can't be broken by distance, or Simanca, or the things that make us different than we were."

Thedra laughed under her breath. "You always could make a good speech, Khe. It was your gift, even before your talent was discovered."

I smiled. "And you, a lovely song, even if your speech was less than warm."

I sat down again, next to Thedra, our shoulders

touching, sisters as we had always been. But there was a lie to it. We could never be sisters again. They were as they always were—but I could never again be the Khe they had loved.

Jit pulled her legs up under herself and hugged her arms to her chest. "Will you tell us what happened?"

I told them about the cruel doumanas who'd thrown rocks at me after I'd left Lunge, about being chased by the beast in the wilderness, and Marnka, the babbler who kept me alive until I came to Chimbalay. I said a side effect of the treatments from Pradat was the reason my spots didn't light. I couldn't bear for my commune-sisters to know the truth. I couldn't tell them what Weast had done to me in that dark room, when it tried to make me spawn an unnatural race. I couldn't tell them what I had become.

-=o=-

"There's no need for you to go." Azlii leaned forward, setting her forearms on the table, bumping the bowl that had held her evening-meal.

"And you shouldn't," Nez said, reaching out to push Azlii's bowl safely away from her angry arms.

"But I promised Simanca an answer," I said. "If we leave without my giving one, she won't traffic with Kelroosh again—that's the way she is. Lunge is too large a commune for us to lose their trade."

"Pftt," Azlii said. "Once you tell her you won't be staying in Lunge, she'll blame 'those corentans in Kelroosh' and won't traffic with us anyway." She leaned further forward. "You are going to tell her 'no' aren't you?"

65

I'd thought over that question since the moment Jit, Stoss, and Thedra had returned to Lunge, and I thought it over again now.

If I didn't go back, Kelroosh would get no provisions.

Simanca didn't want me back in our community out of love. She wanted me in the fields, once more pushing the crops so that Lunge—and she, definitely she—would benefit. Simanca knew any day could be my last. She likely thought she might as well get what she could while she had the chance. Simanca was a cold-necked doumana and I owed her nothing. I'd left Lunge to live the last year of my life under my own control. If I went back now, it would be as if everything that had happened had been for nothing.

Not nothing. With Larta's help, Azlii, Nez, Pradat, and I had stopped the lumani and driven them from our world. The only changes we seemed to have made were now some communes were afraid to decide which crops to grow or what colors to dye their fabrics, and hatchlings were left to die at the mating grounds. It didn't look like an improvement to me.

And there was something else. Lunge was my first community. The place where I'd emerged. Where I'd stayed alone while my sisters went to Resonance, but where I'd also found joy with a hatchling named Han, and discovered myself. I missed the fields and orchards. The structures. Even the nasty-tempered preslets that gave all birds a bad name. Part of my heart would always be at Lunge. I ached to see it one last time and feel its soil beneath my feet. How could I not go?

Azlii scratched her knee idly, her movement pulling me back from my thoughts.

"I've changed my mind," she said. "Khe should go—and offer to stay."

"No!" Nez glared at Azlii. "You would sell Khe, who you claim as sister, for a few handfuls of grain and a gallon of awa juice?"

"Khe should return to Lunge," Azlii said. "We'll get our provisions, and we'll steal her back. Simple."

I stared at Azlii, too. Corentans had their own ways of thinking, but this was impossible. I could never tell that sort of lie.

Nez drew her eyebrow ridges together. "How would we get her out?"

"Have you both turned to babblers?" I said. "I can't break my word if I give it. Nez, you know that's wrong."

Azlii kept her eyes on Nez as she spoke, as though I wasn't there, or was merely furniture, or a crop whose distribution needed to be decided.

"Simanca will send her back to her unit," Azlii said, her voice as confident as if she had already seen the future. "Khe will draw us a picture of Lunge's structures, where everything is. I saw her unitmates when they came yesterday. They feel guilty about how Khe suffered. They feel partially responsible. They won't try to stop us."

"What if they don't keep her with her old unit?" Nez asked.

Azlii thought for a moment. She turned to me. "Can you whistle like a redtail?"

"Finally, the chair is asked in which corner it would

like to be placed," I said. "I thought perhaps you and Nez would decide my fate just between the two of you."

One spot on Azlii's neck fired purple-gray in concern, then winked out. "It's a good plan, Khe, but of course you don't have to do it. You can stay with us. I'd rather you did. We can find food somewhere else."

I crossed my arms over my chest. The truth was, at this time of year, Lunge was likely one of a very few places with enough extra to trade it away.

Azlii leaned toward me. "Once the provisions have been delivered, Nez and I will come for you when everyone is sleeping. If you're not with your unit, I'll start whistling like a redtail. You answer the same way. We'll know where you are."

Redtails were common beastlets around Lunge. This time of year they could keep you up half the night with their distinctive call.

"That's flimsy," Nez said.

"It'll work," Azlii said, "because as selfish as Simanca is, she's not sneaky. She gets what she wants through threats and intimidation, not stealth. No one in Lunge would ever consider that Khe might escape a second time."

Nez was nodding, listening to the plan, and her spots glowed with the white of satisfaction. She reached up and touched her throat. "Good thing Khe's spots no longer light. They won't give her away."

I stared at them both as if I'd never seen them before. I had never seen them before—not likc this, doumanas who wanted me to lie, who schemed to get what they wanted from Simanca without giving up what they wanted to keep. How were they any different from Simanca, who would bend *The Rules of a Good Life* until they broke to get her way? Azlii was corentan, and didn't think as a set-place doumana would. Azlii already thought nothing of getting the best end of a deal, never considering fairness. But Nez was set-place. It wasn't just me the lumani had changed for the worse.

"Do it for the hatchlings," Azlii said, "because in truth, we can't feed them if we don't get provisions now. We'll have to leave them behind."

"Simanca will be glad to have them," I said, though a small twinge shot through me at the thought of leaving them with her.

"She won't," Azlii said. "We both thought she would, but Wall listened to her talking with her unitmates as they were leaving Kelroosh. Simanca said they have too many hatchlings now, with you gone. Unless you come back and push the crops, they won't be able to acquire the new fields they need to give those hatchlings work to do once they emerge. And if there's one thing that's true about our kind, it's that we need something useful to do."

"Simanca thought she'd have me through this year. She made her plans based on that."

Azlii shrugged. "Seems that way. She certainly won't be happy if we try to drop an extra eight hatchlings with her—even if she thinks she has you again."

My lips bent in the weakest of smiles. "Whistle like a redtail. I can do that."

Home sent, *Be very careful, Khe*.

SEVEN

My scalp was sweating as we left Kelroosh for Lunge. I was a commune doumana at my core, and Simanca had been my source of guidance most of my life. I'd come to see that some of *The Rules of a Good Life* were there for the convenience of our leaders, and that some were profoundly true. The Rule that came to me now was 'Betray not those who love you, for the wound to their soul is forever.' I loved so many. Who did I love most?

A fine drizzle fell from a low gray sky. The doumanas of Lunge were gathered at the edge of the commune, spread out in a quiet line, their plain gray cloaks pulled tight against the chill air. I spotted Jit, Stoss, and Thedra. Their eyes locked onto me and didn't let go, but their necks were hidden behind collars since Azlii was with me, and I couldn't see their true feelings. A fallow field lay behind the doumanas—rich, brown soil stretching back to the hub of structures that had been my home. Only the Lunge hatchlings couldn't keep still, bouncing on their feet or weaving side to side from the excitement of it all.

Nez and Azlii walked beside me. Azlii wore her trader's collar and one of the Bethon Blue cloaks she planned to offer Simanca in exchange for extra food. She'd said there was nothing like showing a doumana a luxury to make her begin craving it. I slowed a step. Nez put one hand on my elbow, as if she feared I would fall and wanted to be ready to catch me. I blew out a deep breath and picked up my pace.

I'd expected Simanca to walk out to greet us, but she stood her ground, waiting until we crossed onto Lunge before she drew a smile on her mouth and raised a hand in welcome.

"You have returned to us," she said.

"Yes."

"You've made your sisters very happy today, Khe." She glanced at Azlii. Her eyes focused on and then roamed over the rich cloak that covered the corentan's shoulders. "Come. We have a small feast prepared. We'll eat and then discuss your needs."

I didn't need to see Azlii's neck beneath the collar to know that she, too, had caught Simanca's meaning. Lunge had enough food for a feast. Azlii was the beggar at the table. I was not all the payment Simanca now wanted.

The tables in the communiteria had been pushed together to make one long plank. Simanca led Nez, Azlii and me toward the end furthest from the door. She took the seat at the head and motioned for us to sit to her right. Her unitmates, Tav, Min, and Gintok, took the seats to her left. I looked for Jit, Thedra, and Stoss, craning my neck to see over the doumanas pouring in the doors until I saw them. I wanted my commune unitmates to sit next to me, but those seats were already taken.

I stared down at the table and felt the eyes of all my sisters, those who had been my sisters at Lunge, boring into me. Because Azlii—a corentan—was there, every doumana in the room wore a collar. All except me. There was no reason for me to, and Nez had pointed out that Simanca and the doumanas of Lunge would feel more comfortable and trusting if they thought I had nothing to hide.

But I thought Nez was wrong. It could make my commune-sisters nervous and wary, seeing no emotion spots light on my neck. Just as my unitmates had, my commune-sisters would ask themselves if Khe felt nothing at returning to them. How could she feel nothing? Was something wrong with her? The answer to that question was one I didn't want to give.

I could only hope that Jit, Stoss, and Thedra had already told my story. Simanca would have demanded to know everything that had been said between us, so at least Simanca and her unitmates knew. Had she told everyone, or kept the knowledge to herself?

Simanca looked down the table, caught Thedra's eye, and nodded slightly. Thedra rose. The room went quiet and she pulled herself up tall and began to sing.

Her clear, high voice sailed through the room. She sang a song I hadn't heard before, a song of the land of Lunge stretched out warm and brown in the sun, of the brave new shoots that pushed from it and grew. It seemed that every note came straight to me, wrapping around me like a blanket, enticing me to stay.

Nez nudged my side and shot me a harsh look. I saw her suddenly with lumani eyes—the purple-gray of concern, the muddy-green of jealousy, and the orange-yellow of confusion filling her outline. The gold cord that I saw only between the two of us streamed toward me.

I shifted my glance to Azlii, but she was only herself. When I looked back at Nez, she was herself again, her head slightly cocked, a question in her eyes.

Thedra finished her song and sat down. The doors between the food prep area and the eating room of the communiteria burst open and doumanas pushing food carts came into the room. The sweet scents of kiiku and mern and the sharp spice of truleer filled the room—so strong it was like a fog, something you could almost see. The same unit who'd done this work when I'd lived here did it now. Why would it be any different? I had left Lunge, but life here had gone on as always. I tried not to feel sad.

The sisters rolled the carts up to the long table and doumanas began selecting the dishes they wanted. Conversations started. Azlii kept her head down, eating, looking up only to comment on how delicious everything was. Simanca had been clever. She'd always gone to Kelroosh to trade, traveled into Azlii's territory. Now Azlii had come to her, which gave Simanca the advantage.

Not everyone had finished eating at the long table, but Simanca had. I'd picked at the food on the plate, pretended to eat it. If anyone noticed that my plate was still as full as when the meal had started, no one mentioned it, or eyed my plate and then me.

Simanca pushed back her chair, metal legs scraping across the wood floor, and stood. "Please join my unit at our dwelling," she said to Azlii and Nez—and me by extension. "We can discuss our business there."

Azlii, Nez, and I rose and followed Simanca and her

three unitmates out of the communiteria, and across the small commons. I saw Stoss's eyes following us as we left.

My chest felt squeezed as Simanca opened the door to her dwelling. It looked the same as the last time I'd been there—the walls in the receiving room painted light-green, the furniture and rugs richer than those the rest of Lunge's doumanas had, the visionstage new and large.

The first time I'd been here was when Pradat had come to test me and confirmed my talent to make things grow. I'd come again when the first extra age dot had appeared on my skin. Thirty-five of the dark blue dots lay on my wrist now, but I was not thirty-five. I was thirteen. I wanted to scream the number in Simanca's face.

"Nothing's changed." Simanca spread her hands, silently inviting everyone to sit. "Lunge has the provisions you want," she said to Azlii. "Tell me what you need and what you offer in trade."

I realized that Simanca's "nothing's changed" wasn't directed my way, but at Azlii. Azlii wanted food. Simanca wanted me.

Azlii smiled, and I knew she'd understood exactly what Simanca meant. She shifted in her seat and made a small show of removing the Bethon Blue cloak and laying it across her knees. I watched Simanca's eyes follow Azlii's movements.

"You have three unitmates," Azlii said. "As it happens, I have four cloaks on offer."

Min's, Gintok's, and even Tav's gaze flew to the cloak spread on Azlii's lap. They had likely already reasoned that Azlii would offer it to Simanca. But for each of them to have their own—it was too great a luxury to be given up now that it seemed within their grasp.

I sat with my hands folded in my lap, felt how my neck warmed, and listened to Azlii and Simanca dicker out the trade details. In the end, Azlii had secured enough food to keep Kelroosh, including the eight extra hatchlings, going until Harvest Season. Simanca had promise of five of the seven cloaks—I wondered what she'd do with the extra one—a quantity of meat from the best beastkeeper commune, and a new, small harvester, to be delivered before Harvest Season began. I didn't need to see beneath Azlii's collar to know she felt cheated and used because of the desperate state Kelroosh had fallen into.

I felt something else from Azlii though, a deeper satisfaction. My lumani vision came and I saw Azlii bathed in the ice blue of pleasure in another's woes. She was looking forward to stealing me back from Simanca. That would be her revenge.

Little beads of sweat erupted on my wrists. I didn't like that I half looked forward to it as well. That wasn't the sort of doumana I'd thought myself to be. Except perhaps I was.

The negotiations completed, Azlii, Nez, and I rose to leave. I wanted to visit my old unitmates in the dwelling we'd once shared. It would be my last chance; after Azlii came to get me I'd never set foot on Lunge again.

"Min," Simanca said, "start making arrangements for the goods to be transferred to the corenta." She smiled thinly at Azlii. "We should be able to complete delivery by tomorrow night."

"Our gates will always be open to you," Azlii said.

"Should I go with them to help?" How easily I slipped back into my role as a Lunge doumana, waiting always to serve Simanca's needs.

"Stay, Khe," Simanca said, her voice the most kindly I'd heard it in a long time.

I shrugged goodbye to Azlii and Nez, watched them leave with Min, and waited to hear what Simanca wanted. Tav heaved a loud sigh, rose, and left the room, pulling her collar off as she left. Simanca nodded almost imperceptibly to Gintok, who was standing behind me.

Arms shot around from behind my back, pinning my own arms to my sides. I tried to turn and break free, but Gintok had braced herself somehow and I couldn't move. Her hold tightened. Simanca burst across the room and threw her newly acquired cloak over my head. Bethon Blue filled my eyes. A hand grabbed the cloak at the back of my neck, drawing the fabric close over my face. The fabric was thick. It was hard to breathe.

I twisted and turned and tried to stomp on Gintok's foot, but she was stronger than I would have reckoned, and I had been weakened by what the lumani had done to me. I felt Simanca wrap something around me, rope maybe, pinning my arms to my side more firmly than even Gintok had, and constricting my chest. I gasped, trying to get air. She tied something over my mouth, forcing a fold of the cloak between my lips. Blood pounded in my head. I yelled, but only a strangled sound came out.

My feet left the ground, lifted between them, one taking my shoulders, Gintok—I thought—and the other my feet. They grunted under my weight. I thrashed and made as much noise as I could. One of them yanked hard under my arms and Gintok said, "No use yelling. No use struggling. There's no one to hear. No one to help."

Simanca had planned this. She'd likely sent all the commune doumanas to their dwellings and ordered them to stay inside. She'd have an explanation for my unitmates as to why I hadn't come to see them.

Or were they were in with Simanca on this scheme? A tremble ran across my shoulders.

I heard the door slam shut as I was carried outside. Cool air chilled me where the cloak didn't cover my legs. Thrashing my body was wearing me out. I stopped fighting and let them carry me, saving my strength for the moment when they would have to put me down.

"Upstart little doumana." Gintok's voice, as cold as snow water. "Who do you think you are?"

The sound of running feet. Slap. Slap. Slap. Ragged breath. Azlii? Nez?

"Open the door, Min," Simanca said as we came to a halt.

Grunts. A groan. "It's heavy," Min grumbled.

Hinges, unused to being moved, squealed. Thud of something big and hard hitting dirt.

They set me on my feet and someone loosed whatever bound me. I flung my arms wide, hoping to hit one of them and then run. Min, I guessed from the feel of her hands, grabbed my wrists and pulled them together, pinning them together over my chest. Someone else held my upper arms tight to my body. The cloak still covered my head. I couldn't see where I was.

"Ready?" Simanca said. "Now."

A hard shove in my chest, and I fell through chill air, arms and legs failing. I landed in a heap on a hard surface. I tore at the gag that stopped me from yelling and tied the cloak over my face. Before I could tear it off, I heard a door above me slam shut.

I knew where I was the moment I got free of the cloak. Even in the oily darkness, the smell came to me. Roots—chiva, by the musky scent, harvested before Barren Season and stored for preslet feed during the cold time. There were several root caches on Lunge, but we hadn't come far from Simanca's dwelling. I knew which cache I was in, and how deep it was, how solid and heavy the door that sealed it.

EIGHT

The root cache was cold, damp, and dark. I rolled onto my side and levered up to one elbow. My muscles quivered. I fell back down in the dirt.

I lay exhausted in the dust, wrapped in the Bethon Blue cloak, anger seething through me, and thought about Simanca—what she and her unitmates had done.

Simanca had treated me badly, sending me off to the fields season after season, knowing it was killing me. But it hadn't started that way. She'd brought Pradat to Lunge because of concern for me. She'd set in motion the chain that had let me feel Resonance and mate. It was our duty to mate, to ensure the next generation, but it was more than duty that had driven her, I was sure of that. It was concern. And caring. Now it seemed that half the world had turned into babblers. None but a babbler would throw her sister into a cold, dark cellar and leave her.

Not that she'd keep me here long. She had use for me. She'd leave me just long enough to let me come to my senses, as she saw it. Leave me without companionship, the one thing no commune doumana could stand, until I was happy to work the fields again, if only to be among my sisters. But I had been alone before, long days and nights with none but myself for company when I'd escaped from Lunge, and had survived it. I would survive this hole as well.

Simanca couldn't know I had little need for food or drink, that hunger and thirst wouldn't give her power over me. I could lie in this dank corner of Lunge commune a long time and come out no different than I'd gone in.

There were other things Simanca didn't know about me.

Can you hear me? I sent to the root cellar, and listened for a reply. Maybe it had consciousness, being a hole in the ground lined with stones and small timbers, and having a door, though I wasn't sure how much. Wall was mud, stone, mortar, and a gate—essentially the same thing—and no one would say Wall wasn't aware.

Can you hear me? I sent again. *I need to get out. Can you lift your door?*

Curiosity—I felt that from the ground around me, but as something vague and scattered. No reply came, and the door above didn't so much as creak at its hinges.

Please. Lift your door so that I can leave.

Nothing now. Not even curiosity—as if the cellar had heard my desperate whispers, and decided it was only the wind.

Time stretched out, lost its meaning. Thoughts roiled through my mind, voices that weren't there saying how foolish I'd been to think I could stroll back into Lunge and be loved again, and then walk away, back to my new life in Kelroosh. Azlii and Nez wouldn't come to steal me back until tomorrow night, at the earliest. My commune-sisters could pass by for days and I'd not hear one footfall down here.

My neck burned. I hated the lumani for what they had made me. Hated Simanca for using me up. I'd been a good doumana, obeyed *The Rules*, done what was best for my sisters and my community. But I'd been bad, too—had run off to live my own life under my own command and sought to have my life saved. I'd been punished for it when the lumani made me neither doumana nor lumani, but something in between.

Rain began falling outside—a sudden squall, pelting hard against the wooden door above my head. The door was solid. No water leaked in, but the damp felt stronger, colder. I drew my knees to my chest and wrapped my arms around them, for the warmth of my own body. I tried to sleep. If a chance came for escape, I'd need all my limited energy.

A rumble, like distant thunder, rolled through the cache. I shouldn't be able to hear thunder here, underground, beneath the too-solid door. I braced my arms and managed to stand, surprised I felt strong now—stronger even than when I'd come to Lunge tonight—and listened.

A chill ran across my shoulder blades, an awareness of something that I couldn't quite get hold of. Something that felt wrong. *Worry*. From the cache. My palms began to sweat. If the cache was worried, something was certainly wrong—the rumble new, or out of place, or the first note of something worse coming.

The ground began to shake. My muscles clenched, ready to flee—but there was nowhere to run. The shaking grew, knocking me to the ground, my leg turned at a bad angle. The earth was in convulsion. It rippled and shuddered. Dirt clods and small stones fell from the walls, thudding against the ground. I curled up as tightly as I could and threw my arms over my head for protection as dirt and stones bounced on the roiling floor. The rumble grew louder and the bucking beneath me stronger. The door overhead cracked, sending splinters raining down. A thin timber from the frame that lined the cellar broke off and crashed down a hand's breadth from my eyes.

And then the land was still. I lay panting, my heart beating like running feet. I couldn't make sense of what had happened. The planet shaking like that, it was unheard of. But I'd ridden it out.

The sisters of Lunge commune must have felt it too. The panicked chatter of my sisters running above was loud enough to hear through the cracked door. I almost called out, but kept quiet. If my commune-sisters freed me, I'd only wind up in Simanca's hands again. If they'd all gathered in community hall—the place I thought they'd naturally run to—I might escape.

The thin light of night showed through cracks in the door. The largest slice came at the door's edge. I hoped that light meant the hinges had been knocked loose.

The door was high above my head. I picked up the wrist-sized timber that had fallen, but even standing on my toes the limb was too short to reach the door.

The cache was part full of chiva, a flat-sided root we called *stairs to the sky* for the way they could be stacked in the field at harvesting. I took off the cloak. The sudden cold made me shiver. I laid as many chivas as I could on the cloak and dragged it back to the spot beneath the door. The light was poor, but I could see to stack them straight enough to make a step. When the step was about halfway to my knee, I climbed on it and reached for the door. It was still too high.

I shoveled more chivas on the cloak and dragged them over. I couldn't just keep making the step higher. It would become unstable, and I wouldn't be able to climb onto it. I heard some of my sisters still moving around outside—stragglers, or maybe some who'd already been to Simanca or community hall and had been sent back out. If Simanca sent doumanas to check for damage, I couldn't cross the commune unseen.

I needed to get out of the cache.

I made the first step just a little higher, as high as I thought it could go and still have it be stable. I leaned slightly against the step and it didn't tumble down.

More of my commune-sisters were outside now, calling to each other. "The beastkeep is sound." "There's a big crack in the wall of my dwelling." "The hatchlings are scared but fine."

That was good.

Chiva was hard-skinned and fibrous, used only to feed the preslets. This cache was away from the grain rooms, silos, and gourd keeps. Simanca had planned well. I hoped no one would come to check on the root cache.

It had come to this, to distrust not only Simanca and her unitmates, but all my commune-sisters. Tav, I thought, had walked away rather than help Simanca imprison me, but she hadn't come to set me free.

I shook the thoughts away and concentrated on building a second, shorter step on top of the first one.

When it was done, I put the cloak on and climbed onto the first step. It held firm. I took a breath and stepped up on the higher step. It wobbled. I threw my arms out to keep my balance, but it didn't help. I crashed onto the floor on my back, the breath knocked from my lungs. I lay there a long moment, no thought in my mind—only anger burning through me. I'd been foolish as a hatchling, thinking I could come back to Lunge and be among my sisters again as though the last year had never been. That Simanca would be who I hoped her to be, a caring leader, not who she was. That I, in some way, could still be Khe of Lunge commune.

I rolled on to my side and levered myself up, first to my knees, then to my feet. There was no sound now from the ground above, no calling from sister to sister. I pictured them all huddled in the community hall, trying to make sense of the mad shaking of the settled world.

The fallen timber that had nearly hit me lay close by. I picked it up and again climbed the chiva steps. Sweat stung my eyes. Dirt stuck to my skin. I took a deep breath, centered my weight over my feet, and swung the timber at the door as hard as I could. My arms and shoulders ached, but the sound of the door cracking cheered me. I swung again, howling low—sound adding power to my swing—and swung again, until the door was nothing but splinters hanging on a pitiful frame.

-=o=-

The rain had stopped. Slowly, afraid almost to breathe, I eased my head, shoulders, and arms through the opening and looked around. No one. Palms flat on the ground above the cache, I pulled myself up and out. My forearms, shoulders, and back ached. I would have left the now dirtied and torn cloak for Simanca, but the night was cold. I hunched into myself and ran until I reached the blind of the structures. I hugged the side of Simanca's dwelling, the shadows my friend. The few commune-sisters I saw were heading toward community hall. Lights blazed in the structure. Something had fallen, a chunk of wall, the roof—I couldn't tell. Doumanas were outside, pulling at the chunk, trying to move it. I slunk back into the darkness.

When I reached the corner of Simanca's building, the door swung open. Jit, Stoss, and Thedra, their necks blue-red with anxiety, walked into the night. Our dwelling—their dwelling—lay beyond where I pressed tight against Simanca's wall. They would walk right past me.

"It's not right," I heard Stoss say.

Their footsteps were coming closer. Any moment, they'd round the side and there'd I'd be. I turned and ran, ducking low as I passed a window.

"Khe!" Thedra called, but not loudly—a desperate whisper.

I stopped, turned, and backed away from them, moving through the small open space between Simanca's dwelling and the next. I couldn't think for a moment who lived next to Simanca. Jit, Stoss, and Thedra lived nearly halfway across Lunge. Thedra walked toward me, her steps hard and fast. My feet felt stuck. I looked around wildly, desperate to pick the best direction to run. She took hold of my arm.

"They told us," Thedra whispered in my ear. "Simanca said you never meant to stay with us, despite your promise. She said you'd planned to leave us again, go back to those *corentans*." She practically spat the last word.

Stoss stepped up on my other side. "You told us why you abandoned us before. You had good reasons then. What's your excuse this time?"

My gaze flickered back and forth between my two sisters and out to Jit, who stood apart, staring at us.

"The same," I said. "Look around you. Simanca went a little mad while she had me here to push the crops. She traded for more land and hatchlings than this commune can support. I have eyes. The beast-keep is twice the size it was when I left. Two new silos have gone up. Simanca has promised future crops in trade for those debts. She can't deliver without me. What do you think she has planned?"

Thedra loosened her grip on my arm. She stepped back and rubbed at her nose, thinking.

"Look at this cloak," I said, my voice low. We were out of view of Simanca's windows, but other sisters could come out and see us at any time. I didn't want the sound of voices to draw them. "Bethon Blue. You know what this costs? But Simanca was willing to throw it away to keep me here. She dragged me out of her dwelling and threw me into a root cache. I only got out because the earth shiver broke the boards in the cache's door."

Jit came up and stroked my throat. "I don't care what you did or didn't do Khe. You are our sister."

"Worth being shunned for?" Stoss asked, her voice

knife-edge sharp.

"No one needs to be shunned," I said. "Go to your dwelling. I'll disappear into the darkness and go back to Kelroosh. Simanca will never know you saw me."

"There are no secrets here, Khe," a loud voice said. "Everything is known."

We swung our heads to look where the words had come from. Min and Gintok stood shoulder to shoulder in the dim light.

"Come inside now," Mintok said.

The muddy-brown of fear covered Jit's, Stoss's, and Thedra's necks.

I stepped toward Simanca's unitmates. "These doumanas were just about to bring me to you."

Gintok laughed under her breath. "Your neck should be aglow from the shame of that lie, Khe. Where has your decency gone?" She glanced over her shoulder back toward her shared dwelling. "You will all come now."

-=o=-

Tav was sitting in one of the over-stuffed chairs, her hands in her lap, her eyes on her hands. Simanca was in another chair, her back straight with eager expectation but her face composed in worry. My three commune-sisters stood huddled together, a few steps away from me, their chins sunk toward their chests. I didn't know how Simanca and her unitmates knew we were there in the dark, but it was plain they had known, and that Simanca had sent Gintok and Min to fetch us.

"Thedra," Simanca said, "is everything all right at your dwelling? No damage from the—"

She waved her hand in the air as if it might accidently bump into the word she couldn't find. We had no word for what had happened, the shiver and buckle of the planet. Why have a name for something that never occurs? Had never occurred.

Thedra looked up to answer. "No damage. A bowl fell from a ledge and broke. Nothing else."

Simanca nodded. "Good." She turned her gaze to me, but her words were for my unitmates. "Khe was leaving us again, after promising to stay. I'm very disappointed." She shifted her eyes to Jit, Stoss, and Thedra. "You must be very disappointed as well. Here, your own sister and unitmate seems to return to you, takes our hospitality, *pretends* to love us and want nothing more than to return to her rightful place, but all the while she is conspiring with corentans to take our food, seeds, beasts and fowls—and then abandon us in our time of need."

She paused, waiting for my sisters to speak, but none did.

"There are things you don't know." Simanca swung her gaze back to me. "Lunge has been prosperous. But suddenly we have rain. You know that if the rain keeps up, we won't be able to plant at our usual time. What I'm going to tell you now, only my unitmates have known before this. We traded for this information when Trantal corenta was here." She paused, building up her big moment of revelation. "The Powers, who helped us through all the aspects of our lives, have been destroyed."

My unitmates gasped.

"This doesn't seem to surprise you, Khe," Simanca

said.

I kept my eyes on the commune leader, my gaze as level and searing as hers. "I was in Chimbalay, being treated for my affliction when it happened. There was an explosion. No one knows what caused it."

My neck didn't warm at the lie. What sort of doumana was I becoming that I could bend the truth so easily and without shame?

I felt the eyes of each sister in the room focused on me, but I didn't waver from watching Simanca's face. This was a competition Simanca wouldn't win.

Her gaze finally dropped away. "There is opportunity here for Lunge. With Khe to help grow our crops, Lunge will be positioned as a powerful commune, one that can become First among all others."

The leading commune in any region received the largest seeds, the best fertilizer, the newest machinery, the prize hatchlings. The land of Simanca's dreams came without boundaries.

I turned my arm so that my wrist faced up. "I won't have the time to help you."

"But you will have some," she said. "Commemoration Day is still weeks away. If you go to the beast-keep and bird pens and the seed stockpiles now, you can put the extra growth in them that we will need after you are gone."

A large silence grew in the room. Tav left her chair and stood by the window, leaning against the sill. The window behind her was dark. With her light-red skin and white hipwrap, she stood out in sharp contrast. Her voice, when she spoke, was small and quiet.

"Returning doumanas are never asked to work extra in their last days. Our way is to honor the Returners, and expect nothing from them but the joy of their company."

I wanted to stroke Tav's throat. No one contradicted Simanca. Ever.

The glare Simanca sent toward Tav could have cut through walls.

Thedra took a half step forward and sang a few lines from *The Glory of Returning.*

>*"Praise and honor to she who has given*
>*Her best and her all to the task and her sisters."*

My neck burned with gratitude.

The spots on Simanca's throat flamed with the brown-black of anger. She set her hands on the arms of her chair and started to rise. Jit and Stoss stepped back, but Tav and Thedra stood their place.

A deep rumble rolled through the air. I braced my feet, afraid of what might be coming. The world shook again, more violently this time, throwing Simanca back into her chair and all of us who were standing to the ground. My shoulder banged hard against the wooden floor. Pain radiated down my arm. I heard a terrible sound—like rocks rolling into water. And then a sound I knew too well from Chimbalay—the crack of breaking clearstone in the windows. Shards clattered on the floor.

Thedra, Gin, and Mintok jumped up and ran toward the door that hung loose on its hinges, their arms clutched tight to their chests, their bodies bent forward. Simanca bolted from her chair and followed. Jit lay face down on the ground, her arms over her head, as if that could protect her from the chunks of wall crumbling down. I grabbed her hand and pulled her up, saying, "We have to get out of here now. Come on."

Tav lay on the floor as well—her eyes blinking fast, as though a sudden bright light shone on them. I let go of Jit's hand, turned her around, and shoved her toward the door.

A shard of clearstone jutted from Tav's neck. Blood pooled around the shard and ran down over her shoulder to the floor. I sank down on my heels next to her and lay my hand in her open palm.

She took hold of two of my fingers and faintly squeezed. "Go now."

"Not until you come with me," I said. "I'll help you up."

I could see her fading, her life leaking away.

Wall! Home! I sent. *Can you hear me? We need help at Lunge!*

"Simanca," Tav whispered. "She will use you up. No one can stop her."

"Shoosh now," I said. "Everything will be all right."

Wall! I sent again, desperate for help. There was still no answer.

I eased my hand out of her weak hold and touched the few emotion spots not covered by blood. They were already growing cold.

"You were always my favorite," Tav said. She closed her eyes and breathed no more.

The ground began to roil again, harder this time. The wall beneath the broken windows crumbled like mud on a stream bank. I pulled myself to my feet and stumbled outside.

My commune-sisters had all abandoned their dwellings and stood outside—some stunned and as still as boulders, some running one way, then stopping and running another. Lights shining from doors left open in haste illuminated the open ground. Two walls of the granary had collapsed in almost whole pieces. Some of the sisters ran toward the building, some away.

Simanca yelled, "Everyone out to backfield five. Go now."

Backfield five was in the opposite direction to the boundary land where Kelroosh was waiting.

I ran.

The lights of Lunge grew dim behind me. The voices of my sisters were silenced by distance. I peered through the shallow light to see the outline of Kelroosh on the plain. My pulse jumped in my throat.

The plain was bare. Kelroosh was gone.

NINE

I shook my head, blinked to clear my vision, and looked again. I was near enough that I should be able to make out the walls, maybe even the gate. I sped my steps, but knew it was no use.

Something must have happened, some emergency. Azlii and Nez wouldn't abandon me here. What could have made Kelroosh flee? A prayersong jangled in my head.

See my sisters and keep them from harm
Safely held in your loving arms.

Kelroosh was gone.

I needed a new plan. I'd already walked once between Lunge and Chimbalay—the only place I could think to go for sanctuary. I didn't relish doing it again. At least this time I knew what lay before me. This time, I would be wiser.

Fatigue gripped me. My legs felt as stiff as wood. Last time I'd had provisions, tools, a firestarter. This time I had only the torn and dirtied cloak on my back. It was impossible. I'd never make it to Chimbalay.

The wind was picking up. I heard it in the distance, whooshing over the hills that lay between the plains and the wilderness. I pulled the cloak tight.

The roar of the wind rose. I cocked my head and listened hard. Not wind. I knew this sound. I'd heard

93

it the day the beasts chased me through the wilderness and likely would have ended me if not for that sound and what it meant. I peered through the darkness, hoping I wasn't simply imagining what I wanted to hear. Slowly the thing took shape—dark and rectangular, its stone edges softly rounded—descending slowly from the star-filled sky.

Kelroosh.

-=o=-

"Wall felt it coming," Azlii said.

We sat in Home's receiving room—Azlii, Nez and I, Nez sitting close to me, our knees touching.

"Truth," Azlii said, "the plants felt it first, the way they feel long before we do the magnetic changes in the planet that means Resonance is coming. They sent thought-pictures, but you know how plants are—sometimes it's hard to figure out what they mean. But Wall knew. Not what was wrong, but that something was.

It was horrible, Home sent. *The land was shivering.*

"Wall sent for all of us to run to our dwellings, saying we had to leave," Azlii said. "It had never done that before. Some of us did what was asked, but some stood around, questioning. Wall started to panic, screaming at us in a way I hadn't known it could.

"Everyone jumped to her dwellings then," she said. "Moments later, we rose. No one knew where to go. We circled over Lunge and Hetta communes, and the hills, and over the northern edge of the wilderness. Wild birds and flying beasts were in the air with us. Every single one in the area, I think. We had to swerve to miss flocks that seemed to have no more idea where they were going or why then we did."

Nez touched my neck. "But we never forgot you, Khe. We wouldn't have left you."

I wanted to smile, but couldn't manage it. Fear and sorrow wrapped me as securely as the Bethon Blue cloak Simanca had roped around me.

Azlii said, "When the birds started to settle down, we headed back toward Lunge, to get you. We were coming for you, but you were already here."

I told them then about what had happened at Lunge, about Simanca's dwelling collapsing. About Simanca—and Tav.

Nez stroked my throat. No one spoke for a long, long moment.

"What are we going to do now?" I asked finally.

Rain was splashing against the windows. Azlii rose and stared out at the steady fall of drops, as small and hard as gravel, pinging against the window. She tapped her fingers nervously against the side of her leg.

A dark thought ran through my mind over and over, like a stuck loop on a visionstage:

The world is falling apart.

-=o=-

Binley sucked on her bottom lip—thinking, I supposed, before speaking.

"I inventoried this morning. We'll be out of food in three days. We would have been out by now, but we were lucky with the kiiku and denish this year."

Nez shot me a sharp look that I pretended not to see. I'd used my abilities to push the little patch of kiiku and denish in Kelroosh even though Pradat insisted I should conserve all my strength. I was glad I'd done it. If I'd known then what would be happening now, I would have pushed harder.

"We could try at Grunewald," I said. "The doumanas there might have extra."

Azlii nodded. "They've always had plenty to barter."

Grunewald was the commune Simanca had been desperate to beat in the tenth-year competition, the reason she'd pressed me so hard. The reason I'd not live long enough to see the next Commemoration Day.

I shifted on the cushion where I sat and focused on the sound of Home repeating our conversation to the other structures and doumanas. Soon all of Kelroosh would know exactly where things stood. It was better to listen to Home than follow my thoughts down the dark paths they wanted to go. I'd return to the creator soon enough.

It was there though, every moment—the thought of my Returning—like a bruise I kept poking to see if it still hurt, somehow surprised each time that it did.

Azlii stood and dusted her hands against her thighs. "Grunewald it is. We'll leave in the morning."

-=o=-

Kelroosh slid over the plain, slowing and stopping in the open space just beyond the furthest fields of Grunewald, in the wild spot allotted for corentas. Rain pelted the roofs, windows, streets, and commons. The ground, when we stepped outside, was wet, the soil thick and muddy, raindrops splashing as they hit the saturated soil.

Azlii, Nez, and I pulled up the hoods of our cloaks and drew them tight around our faces. When Binley joined us near the gate, her hood was drawn up the same as ours, and she walked hunched forward.

Wall huffed and heaved to get its gate open, the wood swollen from the rain.

Be careful out there, Wall sent as we passed through the gate. *That ground looks as slippery as a commune doumana's promise.*

The fields were empty as we crossed them. No work could be done in this weather, no plowing or other preparations. The few Barren Season crops that hadn't been harvested lay limp on the ground, rotting from the rain. The sight pained my heart. No grower liked to see crops go to waste.

Grunewald was a large commune, the largest in the region, bigger than Lunge. We crossed field after field, our foot casings squelching in the mud—cold leaking through the soles—before the dwellings and main structures came into view.

"I wonder why they don't turn the lights on," Nez said. "It's dark out here. It must be darker inside."

I turned my head so my earhole faced the structures, but I couldn't hear anything.

When we got closer, Azlii called out, "We've come from Kelroosh to speak with you. Will anyone offer us hospitality?"

I expected lights to turn on, doors to open, but nothing happened.

We made our way to the first structure and banged on the door.

No one answered.

We crossed to the structure next to it, and called out. No response. Azlii leaned against the door. It creaked open slowly, as sticky as our gate had been. We stood a moment, listening, waiting, but no one came to greet us.

"Come on," Azlii cocked her head toward the empty-seeming room.

No commune doumana would ever enter a dwelling without notice. I guessed that kler doumanas had the same rule because Nez hesitated as I did.

Azlii glanced up and shook her head. "Pftt. What's wrong with you two?" She pushed the door open a bit further and she and Binley wriggled inside. Nez and I glanced at each other. I shrugged, and we followed them in.

The dwelling was empty.

"They could be in community hall," I said. If commune doumanas weren't in the fields, or in their dwellings, the hall was the place they were most likely to be.

We went back outside, into the rain. The wind had shifted. The drops pelted us from a sharp angle. I shielded my face with my hand over my eyes and looked around until I spotted the large structure that had to be their community hall.

"This way," I said.

Grunewald's hall was large, big enough to hold two of Kelroosh's Hall, with doors as wide as Home was long, built of high-grade Redstone, polished smooth.

Azlii banged the side of her fist on the stone. "We've come from Kelroosh. Will you offer us hospitality?"

No voice answered. The door stayed shut.

"Do you think they're hiding inside?" Nez asked. "Maybe the shivering world frightened them. They could be making offerings."

Corentans are without faith, and Azlii's patience was running thin. "Let's move this piece of stone and find out."

Probably there was a secret to the door, a balance point that would make it swing as if weightless, but we didn't know the trick. It took all four of us, grunting and sweating—Azlii swearing under her breath—to push it open. Our footsteps echoed as we walked inside. If the doumanas of Grunewald were hiding somewhere, it wasn't here. I saw the thought-grains Azlii sent toward the structure, heard her ask where the doumanas of this commune were, but there was no answer. I didn't know if the structure couldn't hear her or didn't know *how* to answer.

Like the root cache, I thought. My shoulders pulled toward my earholes almost of their own accord as I remembered being trapped and trying hard to talk to the cache, thinking maybe it understood but not being sure.

"We'll check the other structures," Azlii said.

Binley glanced around. "Grunewald is a large commune. There must be over a hundred and fifty doumanas living here."

"So where are they?" Nez asked.

We pried our way into every structure, including the beast-keeps and grain bins. The musty scent of stored seed and straw-strewn floor flowed out to greet us. The only signs of life were six preslets pecking at the fallen seeds around the bases of the silos. My neck was hot with worry. The rain had stopped and we'd all pulled back the hoods of our cloaks. The blue-red of anxiety showed bright on the throats of my three companions.

"There's no one here," Azlii said. "No one."

Nez's spots lit purple-gray with concern. "Why would doumanas desert their commune?"

I shook my head. I couldn't imagine anything that would force my sisters off Lunge.

"Beasts?" Azlii said. "Scared by the world-shiver and running in madness through the commune?"

"The doumanas didn't come this way," I said. "Look around. Where are their footprints? They must have fled south, toward the hills."

We stood a moment, thinking about that, until Binley said, "We should get back to Kelroosh."

Nez, Binley, and I turned to start walking, but Azlii didn't move. She stared at the silos and the preslets.

"Find some carrying bags," she said finally. "As big as you think you can carry full."

I looked at Azlii, expecting to see the brown-green of shame all over her neck—it was theft she was planning, as great a sin as lying. The only color I saw was the ocher of impatience.

"Come on, you three. Get a move on. We'll pay the Grunewald doumanas when they return. But we need food now."

I didn't fault her logic, but couldn't make my feet move. It was Nez who said, "I saw bags inside."

We found the thick, canvas bags and filled five with grain and two with squawking, unhappy preslets. At most it would make a day's full meals, but a day's meals were more than we'd have soon enough if we didn't bring back what we'd found. Still, it didn't feel right to me. I knew Kelroosh needed the food—and once I had stolen food myself in Chimbalay—but this was not something any commune doumana would do to another. To take food. To steal seeds that would be food in the future. It was wrong.

But I wasn't a commune doumana any longer. I was of Kelroosh, though not corentan, and my corenta-sisters needed what lay in those silos.

I could only carry one bag. Nez and Binley carried the other four filled with grain, and Azlii carried the six unruly preslets, struggling to escape the sacks.

Shoosh now, I sent to the preslets, to calm them down. *Shoosh. Shoosh.* I felt the birds settle, but I knew it wouldn't last. *Look at this*, I sent to the birds. *This is where you are going.* I visualized Kelroosh, the preslets running free on the commons and through the village. The bagged birds squirmed, but with anticipation now, not fear.

The four of us struggled under our burdens, heading back across the muddy fields. I kept sending the preslets calming visions, but part of me watched the stiffness in Azlii's and Nez's spines and I knew they were thinking the same thing I was: Where were the doumanas of Grunewald commune?

Azlii came to a sudden stop and pointed toward a structure set away from the others, nearly backed into the hills. "What is that?"

Binley shook her head. Nez shrugged.

"A smokehouse," I said. "For preserving beast-meat. Only the wealthiest farming communes have them. Simanca wanted one for Lunge. She might have won it, too, in the ten-year competition, if I hadn't left."

Azlii kept her eyes on the structure. "Would there be food in there?"

"Maybe. It could all have been eaten by now."

"Let's go see," she said.

The other four started toward the smokehouse, but I said, "Wait. Something's wrong."

Azlii sighed. "Something's wrong in this whole commune. We'll come back and pay for the food, I promise you that."

"No," I said. "See how the building is leaning slightly? Like a big hand pushed it."

Nez squinted her eyes and cocked her head. "A little. Maybe. I can't tell from this distance."

My steps faltered as we walked to the smokehouse. The closer we came to it, the more my neck burned. I set down the sack I was carrying. The structure definitely leaned, but I couldn't see a reason for it. Azlii had sped her steps, impatient with my worries and me. She disappeared around the side of the smokehouse.

When she reappeared moments later, her neck spots glowed gray-red with shock.

"Hurry," she called.

Nez and Binley dropped their sacks and ran, their footprints deep in the mud.

I came around the side of the structure. The hillside behind it had let loose. Mud and rocks had pushed through the back wall. A river of mud filled the smokehouse almost to the rafters.

"I saw a foot," Azlii said, throwing off her cloak. "Someone's in there. Help me."

We dug handfuls and armfuls of mud, throwing them to the sides, the gritty, sticky sludge wet enough to squeeze water from. Azlii reached her first, the doumana whose foot poked from the muck.

We freed the foot past the ankle, up the leg, almost to the knee. Nez had found her other leg and worked to free it. I inched my way up the mud and found her head, digging fast but carefully, hoping there was an air pocket and she might still be alive.

I stared down at the doumana's still face. "You can stop digging."

"But maybe…" Nez said from behind me.

I looked over my shoulder and shook my head.

"We'll get her free anyway," Azlii said, "out of respect."

I dug down around her, moving the mud away from her neck and shoulders. Azlii took one leg, Binley and Nez the other. The ground was slick beneath us. I dug the toes of my foot casings into the mud. Azlii nodded, and they pulled while I lifted and pushed.

The low, gray clouds opened and a sudden hard rain fell.

"Now what?" Binley said. "We can't build a pyre for her, not in this wet."

"We'll have to leave her," Azlii said.

I swung around to face Azlii. "No. Beasts will get at her out in the open. We can take her to the community hall. Her sisters will find her and give her proper treatment when they return."

"I didn't mean to leave her in the open, Khe," Azlii

said. "We'll have to leave her without a proper pyre and ceremony."

"If her sisters were in there with her, they're as Returned as she is," Binley said, glancing around.

My neck grew hotter. Her unitmates would have been with her, at the least. Whatever brought this doumana to the smokehouse, she would have sisters with her, to help.

"We don't have time to dig through for any others who might be here," Azlii said. "It could be days of effort." She glanced over at the sacks we'd left on the ground. "This rain will soak those through. The grain will be ruined.

"Her other sisters left her." Nez's voice was tight. "The ones who hadn't come to the smokehouse. Left, and ran away. How could they do that?"

"They didn't know anyone was here," I said, trying to soothe her.

One spot of soft-yellow-green bloomed on Nez's neck, but her doubt was misplaced. She didn't know commune doumanas the way I did. They wouldn't have left—not if they knew their sisters were in danger."

"Or they tried to save them and couldn't," I said.

Azlii nodded. "Two landslides. Maybe more."

"Where are the rest of them?" Binley asked. "They're not all buried in the smokehouse."

There was no answer to that. Azlii slung her muddy, wet cloak over her arm. "Clear a space and put the sacks in the smokehouse. We'll get this doumana into their community hall and come back for the food. We have sisters of our own we need to help."

Ten

No one spoke on the walk back, each lost in her own thoughts. It was hardest on Nez, I thought, being kler-raised and insulated from the sorts of accidents that happened on a commune. But Nez had been taken by the lumani. She knew about panic and pain. She understood about making hard choices for the greater good.

In Kelroosh we went straight to Home to dry ourselves and get clean garments—and to think. The five grain sacks and two bags of preslets were stowed in a corner of the receiving room. Azlii told Home about the abandoned commune, the mud-filled smokehouse, and the Returned doumana, but asked Home to keep the news to itself for a while, until a decision was reached.

Home sent, *You should tell Community Hall what happened. Between the five of us, we will, I am sure, come to a fine solution.*

"That's a good idea," I said aloud.

Nez looked at me, her lips pulled taut. "Could I be in the conversation too?"

I touched her neck lightly. "Home suggested we bring Community Hall in on the decision-making."

Azlii shook her head. "I've thought it through already. The only solution is the obvious and true one.

We'll take the grain and preslets to the communiteria. We'll tell everyone about the abandoned commune."

"Won't they be upset?" Nez asked.

"Of course they'll be upset," Azlii said, fastening on a dry hipwrap. "Food stores practically gone. Leaders who can hardly decide if they should get up in the morning, much less what supplies they need. All this rain out of season. A planet that is suddenly shaking like a frightened hatchling. And now an abandoned commune. We'll put our sisters right to work getting ready for travel." She ran her hand over her scalp. "The three of us will go to see Larta. Maybe she knows something."

My breath caught in my chest and my neck warmed. "Pradat warned me to stay out of Chimbalay. You and Nez go."

"Really, Khe? The short amount of time you have left and you're going to spend it being afraid to walk into Chimbalay? I'd pegged you for a different sort of doumana than that."

I made a noise that could be interpreted many ways. Sometimes the fact that my spots no longer lit was helpful.

"Besides," Azlii said, "I need you, Khe. Most kler doumanas have never met anyone from a commune. Only you can explain the commune viewpoint so that Larta and I understand."

"I don't like it," Nez said.

I touched each of the lit spots on Nez's neck. "Azlii is right. I don't want to go into Chimbalay and flaunt myself to those who are angry with me, but I can't live what's left of my life being afraid. And I'd very much like to see Larta again."

Azlii clapped her hand against her thigh. "Good. It's decided then." She glanced at the corner where the goods had been left. "Let's get these noisy birds out of here. We should be on the travel before sunset."

-=o=-

"Going up," Azlii said.

An unnecessary warning—the lurch in my stomach had already told me Kelroosh was rising. Nez yelped and grabbed my hand.

"Pftt," Azlii said. "You really should go get your fabric and colored threads, Nez. Something to keep you busy and your mind occupied while we travel."

Azlii could be as blunt as a broken knife.

Kelroosh banked suddenly. Nez leaned so far into the turn she nearly rolled over, and squeezed my hand tightly. I stroked her neck with my free hand.

As quickly as the bank had come, Kelroosh straightened and began to slow. Then it seemed we tilted slightly and began circling.

Kroot kroot, Home sent to get our attention. *Wall says there are doumanas in the hills.*

That old Wall is starting to see things, Azlii sent. *We pass over these hills all the time. No doumanas live there. No doumanas live in any hills anywhere.*

"What's happening?" Nez asked.

"Wall thinks it sees doumanas in the hills," I said.

If Wall says there are doumanas, Home sent, *then there are. Wall is never wrong.*

"Wall did spot the hatchlings," I reminded Azlii.

Azlii rubbed the ridge over her right eye. *Can we set*

107

down? Is there room?

I heard the soft whirring that structures sometimes made to each other—their native language, I presumed, something doumanas couldn't translate.

Wall says there's no flat space big enough, and that Azlii should come take a look for herself.

Azlii sucked in her cheeks. *Do I look like a babbler? The one thing we never do is step outside during travel. The true soil of Kelroosh is too thin to support our weight.*

Home sent, *The soil will move around and thicken under your feet so you don't fall through on the walk.*

Azlii stared at the door, but didn't say or think-talk anything.

Home let out a chuckle—like wind through an empty structure. *Yes, there are things Kelroosh can do that not even corentans know. Come on now. The walk is safe.*

Azlii rose, grabbed her cloak off the peg by the door, and stepped out into the rain. I didn't think Home would send her to do something dangerous, but my neck warmed, and if my spots had lit they would have shown the same blue-red of anxiety that was all over Nez's throat.

When Azlii returned, she tossed her wet cloak on the peg, walked straight over to a large pillow and settled herself on it.

"What did you see?" Nez asked.

"Doumanas, just as Wall said. I recognized a few of them—from Grunewald commune. They saw us circling. Some ran and hid, but others waved their arms. I couldn't hear them, but I know they were calling out to us. Calling for rescue." Azlii sighed. "Wall was right. There was no place to land."

-=o=-

Just coming up to the hills, Home sent. *Then down over the wilderness, and then to settle outside Chimbalay.*

I rubbed my arms, trying to chase away the chill running through me. The last time I'd passed over those hills I'd been on foot, escaping Lunge commune, my home then. I'd climbed the hills and gone down into the wilderness looking for salvation and sanctuary. Instead I'd found beasts, feathered and fanged. In Chimbalay, among the tall buildings and sophisticated doumanas, I'd found other beasts—the lumani, soft spoken and made of energy. Those beasts, the lumani, had changed me, made me what I was now.

Something unwanted in Chimbalay.

Nez sat on a pillow next to me. She reached over and stroked my throat.

"Even if the doumanas in Chimbalay do blame you for the destruction of their energy center, how many actually know what you look like? Hardly any. You could pass right by almost everyone there and they wouldn't know you for who you are. There's nothing to be nervous about."

"But it's my fault," I said. "I destroyed the energy center and the doumanas of Chimbalay nearly starved because they had no energy to cook with and nearly froze to death because they had no energy to keep their dwellings warm."

"Pftt," Azlii said. "Next thing you know, you'll want to take responsibility for the unseasonable rain, too."

I smiled weakly. "Not the rain."

A slight shiver ran down Nez's arms and a soft,

surprised, "Oh," popped out of her mouth. "That's not all that's bothering you, Khe. It's the memories you're afraid of. Of remembering what the lumani did to you."

Home chuckled softly. *That one may be useless at think-talking, but she knows your heart. And she's wise. Wiser than you, sometimes. You should listen to her, Khe.*

Nez rubbed her hand across her face. "It's not only your own memories that frighten you. You're afraid of what I'll remember, what Azlii will feel, walking in that place again.

"We'll be fine," Nez said. "I'm looking forward to being in Chimbalay. It's my place. My first place, at least. Kelroosh is my place now, maybe. For me, I want to walk those streets again. I want to see Mees and my other kler-sisters. I think maybe being in Chimbalay again will help me understand where I truly belong."

Lunge was my 'first place', but returning had brought me no joy or peace. I hoped the outcome would be different for Nez in Chimbalay.

Azlii sighed noisily and pulled herself to her feet. "We've landed. We'll be anchored soon." Her mouth formed a wry smile. "Chimbalay is always an adventure."

-=o=-

The Chimbalay doumanas poured through the high silver gate, gathering bags in hand, making their way to Kelroosh. They were likely delighted the corenta had settled outside their gates so soon again after the last visit—another opportunity to step outside the walls—despite the hard rain pelting their cloak-covered heads.

Beasts roamed the wilderness outside Chimbalay. Unless a doumana was secure in a transportation vehicle or had the safety of a kler or corenta around her, she would never leave.

I saw their happiness at being out. They couldn't see my nervousness about walking in through those gates again.

We angled our way through the crowd, heading in as hundreds streamed out. We wore kler-style cloaks and trading collars and carried gathering bags stuffed mostly with dried stalks but with goods peeking over the rims. The Chimbalayans paid us no mind. We were nothing to them but sisters who'd managed to reach the corenta early and were now returning. Our slow pace, if they noticed, was explained by the abundance of goods we carried.

"It'll be good to see Larta again," Azlii said.

"And Mees," Nez said, her step visibly lightening at the thought of being with her kler-sister. "And the hatchlings. I must talk to Mees about taking the hatchlings we found. They're all female, so the males must have picked up their lot. I'm sure Mees will be happy to have the new ones."

I couldn't see her neck through the collar but was sure it was pale-green with contentment. Chimbalay was her home—her first place, as she'd called it. Just as Lunge was mine, and I'd been happy to see my commune-sisters. Not so happy to see Simanca. But Nez was happy here in this place made by the lumani for their comfort, this place in which both she and I had suffered. She seemed to have made peace with what had been done to us, more so than I had.

111

My stomach knotted as we passed through the main gate. I felt again what I'd felt that night, heard the sounds of metal twisting and windows shattering as the energy center the lumani had selected as the site of their stand-off was destroyed. The building itself had chosen to help, and had been destroyed in the process. I remembered running as metal and clearstone rained down, falling behind as my allies bolted for the gate. I remembered, too, what the lumani had done to me. To Nez. To Inra. I had plenty of reasons to be glad of their destruction.

I pulled my hood closer around my face, making a small fabric cave in which to hide. Nez was right—few doumanas here would recognize me, but it took only one. At least we wouldn't be going all the way to the center ring, where the energy center had been. Where the research center still was, the place where Azlii and Nez had suffered and Inra had been Returned before her time. The place where I'd been turned into whatever sort of thing I was now.

When we reached Guardian House, where Larta lived, Nez nearly ran up the ten steps to the door and stood in front of the spy hole. The walk had tired me. Azlii took my elbow, to help me up the stairs. The door irised open almost immediately and a stiff-backed guardian appeared and waited for someone to speak.

"We're looking for Larta," Nez said.

My chin was tucked into my chest, but I could imagine the bold look Nez was handing the guardian. We were in Nez's world now, and she had taken control.

The guardian's shoulders relaxed. "Larta doesn't

live here any more. She was spending so much time at Justice House that she and a few of her sisters moved on in." The guardian peered at Nez. "Do I know you?"

"I'm Tanez, of Hatchling House Four."

I stiffened, hoping the guardian wouldn't recognize Azlii or me. The truth was, few doumanas of Chimbalay had much love for Azlii either, even before the lumani were destroyed. The collars were the proof of it: set-place doumanas didn't trust corentans any more than corentans trusted them. There could be friendships, but even though Azlii and Larta felt warmly toward each other, there was a gate between them that never fully opened.

"Larta will be glad to see you," the guardian said. "Do you know the way to Justice House?"

"Yes," Nez said. "Thank you."

"Larta isn't merely First of the guardians now," the guardian said. "She's, well, she oversees the kler. Picked up where the powers left off after they were blown to smithereens."

Picked up where the powers left off. I didn't know what to make of that.

The guardian peered hard at Azlii and me, but whatever she felt wasn't strong enough to light her spots. Maybe there were more in Chimbalay without hard feelings toward us than Pradat had led me to believe. Or maybe they blamed me, but not the others. Doumanas weren't always logical.

"Thank you," Nez said again and turned to lead us.

Justice House was in the center ring of Chimbalay, the same ring as the energy and research centers, but on the other side.

"I know a good route," Nez said. "We won't go by… those places."

She strode off. Azlii and I followed like hatchlings.

-=o=-

Larta's neck lit up like a Resonance night sky, spots aglow—yellow-green with surprise, crimson with happiness, white with satisfaction. She stepped out onto the porch, grabbed Nez and Azlii—one with each arm—and pulled them close. Nez and Azlii had removed their collars while coming up the steps. Their necks also glowed with the vivid crimson of happiness. Larta turned them loose and took me by the shoulders, her hands pressing the wet fabric of my cloak.

"Khe. My dear sister, Khe. You look well. I'm very glad to see you again."

Happiness and relief flooded through me. I wished my emotion spots would light, so Larta would know. But she seemed to know anyway, and the crimson on her own neck didn't fade. She looked into my face for a long moment. Her lips tipped in a wide smile as she lifted her hands from my shoulders.

"Well, Tanez," Larta said, turning to her, "I thought you'd gone off forever to be a corentan. You look half-corentan, even in a kler cloak, foot casings, and hipwrap. It's in your bearing."

"Nez is at least half-corentan now," Azlii said. "Corentans are proud with good cause."

Larta laughed. "Of course they are, Azlii. How fine that you're here to remind us of all the reasons. Do come in." She swiveled to the side, giving us room to pass into Justice House. "We have much to talk about."

114

The foyer was probably as big all by itself as the receiving room in Home. The floor was some sort of polished stone—dark-blue-red, the color of curiosity. The door behind us irised closed.

The crimson on Larta's neck winked out. "Things have changed since last you were last here."

A tingle of anticipation slid down my breastbone as we followed her into the receiving room.

I'd forgotten how large rooms like this could be. I'd grown used to the corentan way of living, where a doumana usually had a dwelling to herself and didn't need a receiving room bigger than an area to fit a few sisters. Kler dwellings were like commune living, with whole units sharing the space. I wondered how many sisters Larta lived with here. A great many, I guessed, to need a room this size.

On a clear day light would have poured in from the numerous windows. Today the room was lit by the glow of white globes that lined the ceiling and stretched down the walls between the windows. It wasn't as nice as natural light, but the effect was cheerful. And opulent. I felt uncomfortable, as if none of us belonged in a room like this, a room made to lumani specifications. A room where the lumani had passed judgments, using their doumana surrogates to hide where the true power lay. My neck warmed, nerves tingling, wondering what 'changes' Larta wanted to tell us about.

The main room held three different seating areas, each with a good amount of open space between them. One had two long chairs that faced each other, with single chairs flanking either end. The fabric, oddly for such a room, was plain and serviceable, as it was on all the seating. On either side of the single chairs were small tables, big enough to hold a tumbler and perhaps a small bowl or two but nothing more. The other seating areas were smaller: a set of five single chairs in a circle with a round clearstone-topped table in the middle, and a set of three chairs in a triangle, each with a small wooden table between them. The smooth walls were painted the pale-green of contentment, like many of the rooms I'd seen in Chimbalay. I thought a truer choice would have been the bright-green of pride.

Larta took a seat at the five single-chair setup and gestured with her chin for us to sit.

"Kelroosh wasn't due at Chimbalay again until after First Warmth," she said. "What brings you here early?"

Azlii shrugged. "As you said, things have changed. And not all for the better."

Larta set her elbows on her knees, her chin on the ledge of her two fists.

Azlii leaned forward, as if to speak, then sat back. The blue-red of anxiety blossomed on her neck. She leaned forward again and tucked her hands between her knees.

"The truth is, Larta, I need a favor. A large one. Kelroosh is nearly out of food. We managed to secure some at Grunewald, but we're going to need more soon. I need to barter with you." She looked up. "I hope you have some to spare."

I focused my gaze on Azlii's throat to see if her neck showed shame at having stolen the food at Grunewald, at lying to Larta about how we got it. There was nothing more on Azlii's neck than a couple of spots lit with the purple-gray of concern—for her sisters in Kelroosh, I thought.

Larta laughed. "Corentans! Such misplaced pride. We have our differences of opinion, Azlii, but I count you as a sister. I'll send word to our doumana in charge of foodstuffs. You'll have what you need."

Azlii blew out a breath. "Our doumana in charge is called Binley. Tell me where to send her and she'll be there."

Larta tapped on the slim textbox she wore at on her left forearm—just above her age dots—then turned back to Azlii. "Tell me what other news you have. Communications with other klers and the communes have been spotty since the incident with the energy center."

I looked down at my feet. Everything we do has repercussions, mostly ones we don't guess at ahead of time.

Azlii told her about the two communes we'd visited. "Wall says it's been in contact with the structures of Jeldish corenta, and they tell similar stories of the communes they've visited. They're stuck, the commune doumanas. They need to make decisions but can't; they've forgotten how."

Larta straightened her back and nodded. "It's been different here, too. There's an odd discontent. I feel it in the streets. You know I'm no empath—if I'm aware, it must be as thick as paste in the air. Some of it we brought on ourselves when we invited a few males to stay in Chimbalay. You wouldn't think that would make a difference, that they'd be just like doumanas but different looking, but they're not like us at all. They stay shut up in their own little world, rarely venturing out. When they do, it's such a rare sight that doumanas stare at them. Then they jump back into their hidey holes again."

"If doumanas hardly ever see them, what difference does it make if they're here or not?" Nez asked.

Larta sighed. "They're different. They make music all the time, and their neighbors complain. I've heard it and I don't blame them. It's loud and raucous, not pleasant at all."

"They look so delicate with their bird-like hand and slender chests," Nez said. "You'd think they'd make music like wind across reeds."

Larta shrugged. "But really, it's not the males. It's something else. Something indefinable. Doumanas argue at the granaries and distribution centers. We used to be happy with what we had. Now this one wants what that one has, and that one wants something else again. We've had theft. Theft! Can you imagine? Not from need, but out of greed. In all the time I can remember, we've had maybe three or four shunnings in Chimbalay. Now we have at least one a week."

"Why would our sisters want more than their share?" Nez said. "What good is more than you need?"

I wondered if the problems in the kler had the same origin as the problems in the communes but had a different effect here.

"There's no hand at the fire any more," I said. "Now doumanas see possibilities and they want as many as they can grab. It's a kind of madness."

Larta tilted her head. "What we need," she said, "is the return of the powers."

ELEVEN

"*Not* the lumani," Larta said, smiling at the massed gray-red spots of shock that sparked on Azlii's and Nez's necks. "No one wants them back. But there seems to be a need for some sort of centralized planners, some centralized control."

"To decide what colors fabric should be dyed?" Azlii scoffed. "Not a job I'd relish."

A story Azlii had told me bubbled in my memory. "It's like in the Before. When the lumani came, they made chaos. To end the chaos, doumanas and males were willing to give up their old lives and be ruled by the Powers—accepting anything to have stability again."

"Except corentans," Azlii said.

I nodded. "Those who wouldn't bend to the new order gave life to those who are corentans now. Those who did bend became kler and commune dwellers. But that's not the point. My commune-sister, Thedra, once said we're like flocking birds. We want a leader to follow. Even corentans want that. Larta is right. We need a return of the powers."

Silence stretched out in the room, so complete that one without eyes would believe the space empty. I let it linger, giving my sisters the time they needed to reason it through. I thought about Simanca, who had no problem making the decision to lock me in the root cache like an errant preslet, even though I'd agreed to stay at Lunge. She wanted to make sure, I suppose. And, since Azlii planned to steal me back, Simanca had been right, in a way.

Was Simanca's firm and cruel decision the other side of the rock from commune leaders who couldn't make a choice about anything? Did Simanca, with her love of *The Rules*, believe that with the lumani gone there were no rules at all? Or maybe the rules now were whatever she wanted them to be. If she felt that way, there were bound to be others who did too.

"Maybe," Nez said finally, "something more like a school, to teach doumanas how to make these decisions for themselves."

"Run by corentans," Azlii said, "since we seem to be the only ones who know how to make up our own minds about things."

"Trah," Larta said. "I doubt you'd find many kler or commune doumanas willing to take lessons from corentans. You aren't all that highly thought of among certain segments of the populations—and by that I mean nearly everyone who isn't corentan."

Azlii's lips crinkled. "Set-placers are bound to be jealous of those who live free."

Larta rolled her eyes. But I wondered if there was more than a little truth in that. From the brief time I'd spent in Chimbalay I knew that kler doumanas looked down on commune dwellers as 'laborers' and that corentans did think less of 'set-placers.' Commune doumanas had their own prejudices against both kler and corenta dwellers—thinking the first one spoiled from a too-easy life and the second only slightly more sane than a babbler, and with thievery in her heart.

"What you need," I said slowly "is a council formed from the three ways of living—kler, commune, and corenta. Maybe two or three from each. A council of equals that can sort out problems and help set us all in a new direction for our new lives. The council can meet here, in Chimbalay, at least at first. Maybe later meetings could rotate among sites, so no one feels slighted."

"Pftt." Azlii flicked her wrist. "You think kler and commune doumanas even think that way? Seems to me they only want someone to tell them what to do."

Nez's throat colored brown-purple. "Who is sitting here with you now? Two kler doumanas and a commune doumana who risked everything *not* to be told what to think or how to live." She leaned forward, more spots lighting as her anger and indignation rose. "I'll tell you something—we are not that unusual. You think everyone who isn't corentan happily moves through her life without thought, mindlessly obeying her leaders and *The Rules*? What arrogance. There would be no shunning if no one ever went out of step. There would be no inventions, no change—but there are. There would be no leaders or Firsts, but every commune and kler has them. That we find joy in serving our community and our sisters doesn't make us mindless; it makes us purposeful."

Azlii rubbed her chin. Two spots lit greenish-orange in amazement, surprised by Nez's outburst, no doubt. "I go by what I see. If every doumana is so singular in her thinking, explain what we saw at Two-ling and the weavers' commune—why those doumanas could not make the most simple decision on their own?"

The bright hues of Nez's emotions faded on her neck, but didn't wink out. "Some of us have a harder time making decisions. That doesn't mean doumanas can't be found who could serve well on this council."

I liked that Nez was worked up, the colors bright on her neck. She had held in too much for too long. I'd thought Nez was at peace with what had been done to her, but saw now that she was simply better at hiding it. Nez and Azlii were both right about doumanas in general—but Nez was more right, I thought. I remembered Hwanta, at Lunge commune when I was younger, who raged against her Returning, and Pradat, thwarting the lumani in her own quiet way. And Larta with her secret allies—Nez, Mees, Inra, and others— plotting with Azlii to drive out the lumani long before I'd met them. And Tav and Thedra, choosing to stand against Simanca.

My neck warmed, thinking of Tav. Of watching the bright shine of her life force fade.

Larta had kept her eyes on me the whole time Nez and Azlii were talking, her look as sharp as ice. "What *you* need," she said, her voice harsh, leaning forward and peering at me.

"What?"

"You said, 'What *you* need,'" she said. "As if Khe, herself, were outside what is happening in our world. But you should be on this council."

I shrank down in my chair at the enormity of what I had suggested. This council would be responsible for leading the doumanas toward a new way of living. So much could go wrong. There were so many opportunities for error. I didn't know if I could live with the responsibility—not after the hardships I'd caused with the destruction of the lumani.

"Nez and Azlii maybe. And certainly you, Larta. But not me."

Not me, because I was not soumyo any more, not a member of our kind at all. I had no right to make decisions when my thoughts were now as much lumani as anything else. I was not to be trusted.

Azlii rubbed her hand over her skull. "But it should be you, Khe. And Nez. You two are in unique positions, commune-emerged and kler-emerged but living for the last year in a corenta, you have a feel for both. I can't think of anyone else who can more or less straddle all three."

"Besides," Larta added, "it was your idea. You should be responsible for its execution. Easy enough to be full of ideas if you don't have to be the one implementing them."

A new thought struck me.

"What about the males?" I asked. "They must be running into the same problems. Shouldn't they be invited to have their say?"

Azlii and Larta looked at each other, and both shrugged.

"I suppose so," Larta said

I could see they were uncomfortable with the idea—males being nearly as foreign to us as the lumani had been. But my sisters would try, and that was what mattered.

Larta stood. "There're things I have to go and take

care of. Please, stay here tonight. We can talk more later, and tomorrow."

It felt like a fresh breeze had just blown into the room, pushing away the heavy air that had weighed on our shoulders. No one wanted to go on with this talk just now.

"I'd like to go to Hatchling House Four," Nez said, "to see my sisters."

Azlii pulled herself to her feet. "I'll go with you. I've missed Mees, and her cooking."

-=o=-

"The lumani had Justice House built," Larta told us at morning meal the next day.

Nez and Azlii, so long on partial rations, kept spooning in the vero and barely looked up. Larta had my full attention, at least.

"All of Chimbalay was built to their specifications," she said, "but Justice House, Energy Center, Research Centers One and Three, and a few other places, they designed and had built specifically for themselves, not for doumanas. I guess that's why the rooms are so large. And why there's a little energy center built into the top floors. I don't know what they did here, but it's nice for us." The faint orange of embarrassment showed on her neck. She drained the last of her drink, got to her feet and went to refill her tumbler.

"Larta doesn't need to be embarrassed that she's in this fine building," Nez said.

Azlii tilted her head a bit to the side. "What makes you think she's embarrassed?"

"Color came up on her spots. Faint, but certainly

there."

"Not that I saw," Azlii said. "I don't think she's embarrassed at all. I think she thinks the grand surroundings suit her."

Corentans were supposed to be more sensitive to the subtle colors that showed hidden or suppressed emotions. That was why kler and commune doumanas wore collars when they went to the corenta to trade, so even the subtlest hues wouldn't be seen.

Larta returned and settled herself in a chair.

"How did you wind up here?" I arced my arm to indicate the room and, by extension, Justice House.

Larta ran her hand over the top of her head. "After the explosions, when the energy center was nothing but ashes, clearstone shards, and twisted metal, the doumanas here were fearful. Could it happen again, in some other part of Chimbalay? How did they know the lumani were really gone? What if they weren't, and wanted revenge?

"Doumanas were afraid to leave their dwellings, in fear that something even worse might happen. Nothing was getting done. As First of the guardians I organized patrols to walk the streets all day and all night. I wanted doumanas to be able to look out their windows and have a pretty good chance of seeing a guardian patrol passing by. I sent in 'kind persuaders' to bring doumanas who wanted to hide in their dwellings out and to their assigned work. If Chimbalay didn't function properly, things would get bad in a hurry. I even got in touch with the next corenta due here and convinced them to come early. I wanted a pleasant distraction for the doumanas, to take their minds off what had happened and to show them that life was still as it always had been."

Except that it wasn't, I thought. Life in Chimbalay would never again be as it was.

"No one trusted the doumanas who'd been associated with the Powers," Larta said, "especially orindles, technicians, and those who'd spoken on the lumani's behalf, so doumanas started coming to me with little problems. It began to make sense for me to be at Justice House full time. It was odd. No one wanted anything to do with the doumanas who'd worked with the lumani, but everyone wanted to keep coming to Justice House to solve their problems, just as they'd always done."

"No one blamed you for what had happened to the energy center and the lumani?" I asked.

It hadn't been our wish to destroy the energy center. The lumani had chosen the site, shutting themselves inside to devour the power they consumed as we did grains and fruits. The energy center made the final choice, helping us destroy the lumani, though it meant destroying itself in the process. But the doumanas of Chimbalay didn't know that. How could they when they had no sense that structures could make their own decisions?

Larta pressed her lips together and then blew out a long breath. "You got the blame, Khe. You and Azlii— the strangers. The ones who weren't of this place. You two were seen running from the energy center as it exploded. Pradat and I were running, too, but no one thought anything about that. A good number of doumanas were running for the gates that night—

nothing odd about Pradat and I being in the crowd. But you two, any bad thing that happened must be your fault."

I glanced at Azlii, and laughed. Her neck showed the bright-green of pride. Larta saw it, too, and rolled her eyes.

"Somehow," Larta said, picking up the string of her story, "I wound up basically in charge of everything. I don't like it, but I'm a guardian; it's my duty. Whenever I find a doumana who seems particularly good at overseeing some aspect of the day-to-day running of Chimbalay, I put her in charge and follow what she's doing by reports. I can't wait to find enough doumanas to be rid of all this extra weight."

Azlii gently touched Larta's throat, then sat back.

"Let's start with numbers for the council," she said. "How many?"

"Six seems right, two from each community type," Larta said.

"Twelve," Nez said. "Don't forget the males."

Larta laughed under her breath. "I did forget them. Twelve, then."

"What about Khe?" Nez asked, and they all turned and looked at me.

I reached over and stroked her neck. Her skin was warm with emotion. "No, Nez. Because…" I turned over my arm so that my forearm faced up, "I could Return tonight, or tomorrow or next week." I felt a stone form in my chest. "Commemoration Day is only weeks away. I'll be fortunate to see the Council's first meeting."

Every spot on Nez's neck burned with the pale-blue

of despair. A deep silence settled over the room.

Azlii cleared her throat. "We'll have to narrow things down some. We don't have the luxury of time. I say, two from Kelroosh, two from Lunge commune—don't frown, Khe. Thanks to you, Lunge is now second in prestige only to Grunewald, and who knows what's happening to those doumanas since they scattered to the hills? It has to be Lunge. And two from Chimbalay."

"Better to spread things out," Larta said. "Doumanas who've lived their lives together are likely to have a too-close harmony of thoughts. We want as many different ideas as possible, so we can choose the best. One from Chimbalay and one from another kler. One from Kelroosh, one from another corenta. One from Lunge, one from another commune. The same with the males."

Nez nodded. "But that leaves either me or Larta out, since we are both from Chimbalay."

"Trah," Azlii said. "That won't work. You want to spread out the corenta and commune choices, that's fine, but we need both of you."

Nez squirmed in her seat, but I saw Larta nodding. The decision was made.

"We haven't been idle since that night," Larta said, meaning the night the lumani were destroyed. "We figured a way to direct visionstage presentations to any single site or to multiple sites as we choose."

Nez and I gaped at her. Visionstage presentations went to all klers and communes at the same time. It ensured harmony of knowledge among all doumanas. Once, I wouldn't have been able to imagine a presentation going to some but not all.

"Was that your idea?" Nez asked Larta.

"My idea, but the technicians at Presentation House worked out how to do it. It's surprising what we can do when presented with a problem to solve, especially when the technicians are anxious to prove they weren't the lumani's creatures after all. So we can send a message to Lunge and another commune without it going to everyone. Corentans don't have visionstages, so we'll have to figure another way to reach them."

Nez cleared her throat. "Maybe we should have an empath on the Council. Someone who can see hidden truths."

I wished she hadn't said anything about an empath, and I saw that Nez was sorry, too. The soft-gray of sorrow was alight on her throat. I knew she was thinking again of Inra, her sister at the hatchling house and an empath. Inra, who was Returned by the lumani.

"Or a weather-prophet," Larta said. "Weather-prophets are empaths, from what I've seen of them. They say they taste the upcoming weather, but that doesn't make sense. I think it's more like what Azlii says about corenta structures: that they're in tune with the planet."

I thought of Marnka, a weather-prophet turned babbler, as much a victim of the lumani as I was. She'd saved me in the wilderness, and I had all but abandoned her. I promised myself that I'd find her soon.

Azlii shrugged. "It'd have to be male. All the doumana weather-prophets have been turned to babblers, unless some are hiding somewhere we don't know about. We'll have to hope there are male weather-prophets who are still sane."

"Male then, if we can find some who are." Larta's guardian bracelets slid down her wrists as she made a note on the textbox on her forearm. "And if we can reach them. Males don't get the same visionstage presentations doumanas do."

"The corentas can do it," Azlii said. "The structures all talk, the doumana and male corentas. I'll speak to Wall and have it get the word out. The male corentans can tell each kler and commune as they reach them."

"That's too slow," Larta said.

Azlii flicked her wrist. "Not slow at all. I'd guess that it could be done in under eight days. Of course I can't say how long it would take after that for the males to pick their representatives. We'll have to set a date and give them a deadline or it might never get done."

Larta stood, stretched her arms over her head, and sighed. "I'll speak with the technicians. The invitations will start going out tomorrow."

-=o=-

The guardian who knocked at the door that evening was small, with pale-red skin and tiny eyes. She wore her cloak drawn up tight around her throat, so her emotion spots weren't visible, and rocked from foot to foot before she spoke. I'd heard the things being said, and knew some of the guardians were unhappy I was in Chimbalay, in Justice House. They blamed me for what they'd suffered after the energy center was destroyed.

"The orindle, Pradat, is here and would like to speak

with Khe," the timid guardian said. I wondered how she'd gotten her assignment—most guardians were bold in presenting themselves. "She's waiting in the small courtyard behind. I'll show you the way."

Azlii raised her eyebrow ridges. Nez pressed her lips tight together. I shrugged, grabbed my cloak from the peg by the door and followed the little guardian down the hallway. The passage was lit now even though it was day, the dark clouds outside blocking what natural sunlight usually came through the many windows.

She walked ahead, not beside me, and only looked back when she pointed and said, "Straight that way and out the orange door."

I saw her suddenly with lumani eyes, the blue-red of nerves rising like steam from her shoulders. Was she afraid of me, or should I fear what lay beyond the orange door?

Outside, the air was heavy with mist. Pradat, wearing a hipwrap and foot casings but no cloak, stood under the shelter of a tree, its thick purple and red leaves forming a canopy as solid as a stone roof. Rain could stream like water from a tap and we'd stay dry.

Pradat stroked my neck when I reached her.

"How are you, Khe?"

I pulled my arms out from beneath the cloak, turned my left arm over, palm up, and displayed the thirty-five age dots showing there.

"I thought," I said, hope leaping up in me, "when I looked at my arm this morning, the dots maybe seemed a little lighter in color."

Pradat bent over and peered at my skin. "Perhaps. The light isn't good enough here for me to tell. I'd like

131

to give you another treatment tomorrow, if you feel up to it."

I didn't need her spots to light to know she was thinking about what had happened at the last treatment nearly as hard as I was. That day had shown me my future too clearly—the pyre on which I would rest before Commemoration Day returned.

"I'll be in Chimbalay a while," I said. "I can come any day you want. As many days as you want."

Pradat nodded, but said, "It may not be wise for you to stay in the kler."

"Because the doumanas blame me for what happened."

A cold gust blew through the courtyard. "Do you want to come inside where it's warmer, Pradat? You don't have a cloak."

She gave a small shake of her head. "Some doumanas do blame you for the destruction of Energy Center, others for the destruction of their comfortable lives. With the lumani gone there has been some chaos."

"I know. Azlii thinks things are going to go bad very quickly. We've been talking about—"

The clouds opened and rain fell, hard, fast, and cold. Pradat shivered.

"Please come inside," I said.

She shook her head again. "I don't want to risk what I've come to tell you being overheard."

Rain splattered in the dirt outside the protection of the tree. I pulled my cloak tight over my chest.

"I know about the idea for a council," she said.

It didn't seem like Pradat to be hurt or jealous over

not being invited onto the council, but I'd seen doumanas get upset over lesser things.

"It's my sister-orindles," she said. "Some aren't happy with the idea of a council making decisions for them. The lumani, of course, had things they wanted us to do." She shivered slightly—but not from the cold, I thought. "But largely we were left alone. With the lumani gone, the orindles were free to go in whatever direction interested them. They worry this *council* won't understand our work and will put a stop to much of it. They worry the council will order us to do things that waste time."

"There will be orindles on the council," I said. "Males, but orindles. We would have asked you, but the way the makeup worked out, the slots for Chimbalay were full."

Pradat drew in a deep breath. "My sister-orindles aren't hoping for a spot on the council. They want there to be no council. They want to be the ones in charge."

TWELVE

Larta's hands squeezed the arms of her chair as I'd told her what Pradat had said. "Then we have to hurry." She levered herself to her feet and began pacing a tight circle in the large room. "Once all the council members are chosen and here, there won't be anything the orindles can do to stop us. We need to go to Presentation House now, get the word out, put things in motion." She stopped and shook her head, as if trying to shake out the thoughts lodged there. "Has the entire world turned babbler? The orindles are our sisters. If they were worried, why not come here and speak about it?"

Azlii rubbed her chin, her hand sawing back and forth. "The structures say it was like this when the lumani first came—sisters turning on sisters. Uncertainty breeds fear. The sooner some organization is in place, the better."

I had a thought to add, but it flitted through me and fled. My stomach tightened. A strange smell filled my nose and I heard distant voices—no, one voice, far away, unhappy. Frightened. Pained. And a rumbling, deep and low beneath my feet.

"Trah!" Larta yelled, and grabbed for a chair but missed and was thrown to the floor, the walls shivering, the floor suddenly alive beneath us. I grabbed for Nez, catching her upper arm. Her eyes widened and her neck glowed with the muddy-brown of fear. The same color was on Azlii's and Larta's necks.

It was gone so quickly that if we weren't all sprawled on the ground, I might have thought it hadn't really happened. Larta pulled herself to her feet, crossed the few steps to a chair and collapsed into it. I let go of Nez's arm. No one spoke. The sky opened and rain poured down, beating loudly against the windows.

Did you hear it? I sent to Azlii, not trusting myself to speak.

She nodded. *The rumble. Like a hillside parting from itself, rocks tumbling.*

That, I sent. *But did you hear the voice? Someone was hurt and very afraid.*

"Maybe it was Larta," Azlii said aloud, obviously trying for a joke.

No, I sent. *It was far away. Almost… underneath.*

Azlii shook her head.

Larta sent Azlii a hard look and stood up. "We need to go to Presentation House and call for council members now. The sooner this is done, the better."

-=o=-

The fierce rain, and likely the sudden shiver of the world, seemed to have driven the doumanas of Chimbalay indoors. The streets were nearly deserted as we made our way to Presentation House. We walked with our heads down to keep the rain out of our eyes. Maybe Pradat's treatments were working—I was able to keep up with my sisters. Or maybe it was fear driving me. Fear, and the echo of that frightened voice in my

135

head. I couldn't shake the feeling that the voice wanted me to help it. But how could I help when I didn't know who or what was asking, or what the problem could be?

"You're sure the technicians will let you make a presentation?" Azlii asked Larta.

She blew out a breath. "I'm First of Chimbalay now. There won't be any problem."

The bright-green of pride bloomed on her neck and then was gone, replaced with the orange of embarrassment. The others couldn't see the colors, not through the hooded cloak pulled so tightly around her, but I saw it with my lumani eyes. I wanted to reach out and stroke her throat. It was a strange place Larta had found herself in—a situation she'd not asked for but had embraced. I understood both her emotions. *The Rules of a Good Life* say, "To serve our sisters is the glory of our lives" but I'd long since learned the foolishness and lie of that. We took pride in ourselves, our accomplishments. Why shouldn't we?

The three cold and wet guardians huddled at the doors to Presentation House pulled their backs straight when they saw Larta was in our group. One rushed to open the tall wooden doors.

Larta stopped before crossing the threshold. "How long have you three been on post?"

"Since just after morning meal," a guardian said.

"Before this rain started," Larta said. "Why didn't you call for cloaks? You must be freezing."

"We did," the guardian said, "but no one has come."

Larta tsked and undid the fastenings of her cloak.

136

She held it out it to the guardian. "Here. It's wet on the outside, but it'll keep you warmer."

Nez unfastened her own cloak even as the guardian at the door was reaching for Larta's. Azlii had hers off as well, and gave it to the third guardian. I felt odd, the only one still in the cloak she'd walked over in; the only one who would be warm and dry when we left, if the rain kept falling. I was sure Larta, Azlii, and Nez wouldn't ask for theirs back, and there was no way to share one cloak among the four of us.

The lights were on inside here, as they'd been at Justice House—a poor substitute for the bright sunlight this time of year usually provided.

"Where is everyone?" Larta whispered, mostly to herself, as we crossed the wide foyer.

She asked the question again, this time of a lone doumana standing in the receiving area.

"Trying to get things working again," the doumana said. "The shaking made things fall. Some of our equipment was damaged."

Larta muttered under her breath so softly that even with lumani hearing I couldn't catch her words. She shaped her lips into a smile and said, "Thank you. We'll go and see if we can lend a hand. Where, exactly, is everyone?"

"I'll show you to the others," the doumana said.

She led us down a series of hallways until we reached a door painted the dark-blue-red of curiosity. A fitting color, I thought, given that the visionstage presentations sent from here were meant to educate.

The doumana creaked the door open and then scuttled back down the hall.

137

The room was a busy nest of activity, but it didn't seem these doumanas were trying to fix things. They were walking to and fro, heads bent over textboxes, but not doing anything that seemed at all useful.

A medium-sized technician with dark-red skin and eyes as dark as river-muck stopped and looked up at us. "Welcome."

"Jonton," Larta said, clearly confused. "What are you doing here?"

Nez grabbed my arm. "I know Jonton. She's no technician. She's an orindle."

-=o=-

Jonton swept her palm up in a welcoming arc. "Please, come sit. Take some warm refreshment. This rain has made everyone feel cold." She nodded to a doumana who quickly disappeared through a door at the back.

The room was made for presentations, filled with equipment large and small that meant nothing to me. There were tables covered with textboxes. I could see symbols and script scrolling over the faces. Several hard, straight-back chairs sat tucked under the tables or pulled out and left askew, as though the doumanas who had occupied them had left in a hurry. There was a small raised dais strewn with the traditional flowers of Emergence Day, reminding me how close we were to it. Emergence, then Commemoration, and thirty-five dots on my wrist.

"Shall I have your cloak dried for you while we talk?" Jonton asked, reaching toward me as if to remove my garment herself.

The purple-gray of concern colored Larta's neck, but I wasn't sure what, exactly, bothered her. Jonton's neck was exposed for all to see. The only colors she showed were faint blushes of the crimson of happiness and the greenish-blue of hope. Colors that—as an orindle—she chose to show. Colors that could have meant so many things.

"Thank you," I said as I undid the cloak fastenings and slipped it off my shoulders. Azlii and Nez kept their eyes focused on Jonton as she handed my cloak to someone who I guessed was also an orindle, though she could have been some sort of aide. None wore the green hipwraps that were standard for orindles or the yellow wraps of helphands. Instead they wore brown—a color that didn't describe a position in Chimbalay.

What's your guess? Azlii sent, as the second doumana walked away with my cloak.

I don't know. Kler ways are a mystery to me. At Lunge, this would be considered good manners.

Azlii scratched her neck. *The brown hipwraps?*

A disguise? To what purpose?

I wished we could ask Larta. Something was bothering her, but I didn't know what.

The door at the back opened and the doumana sent to fetch warm drinks returned with a rolling cart carrying a wide, covered bowl with steam curling from beneath the lid, and several cups. The drink's woody yet sweet scent floated through the room. The doumana didn't come toward us, but went across the back of the room to another door that irised open at her approach, revealing a room behind it. She pushed the cart through and was lost to our sight.

"Join me," Jonton said, and walked toward the opened door.

The room beyond was large, and warm—not chilled like the room with the equipment. Several long chairs faced each other in a square, with a large, low table in the center. The doumana sent to fetch refreshments had set the steaming bowl and cups on the table and disappeared again. So many doors in Presentation House. Doors that meant rooms and hallways, and confusion perhaps for anyone trying to find her way out.

Jonton dipped a cup into the bowl, drew the cup to her lips and sipped.

"Mmm." She lowered her cup. "It's very good. Please help yourselves."

The warm cup felt good in my hands. I took a tiny sip of the drink. It was fruitier in taste than in smell, and overly sweet. Larta must have been thirsty, because she gulped her first cupful down and dipped in for a second. Azlii and Nez sipped more slowly, but I could see they were enjoying it. I felt a pang of regret that food and drink no longer brought me pleasure.

"Let us talk about this council idea of yours," Jonton said.

I couldn't tell if her statement was meant to surprise us, or to show that she knew that we were aware the orindles were against the scheme.

Larta set down her cup. "It's no secret there's been confusion among the doumanas since the Powers left. This corentan—" she motioned vaguely toward Azlii without giving her name, "has visited several

140

communes where the leaders are at a loss as to what to do now, without direction from the Powers. The corentans feel that we may find ourselves with a shortage of food, clothing, and other necessities if order isn't restored. Our idea is to form a council from among kler, corenta, and commune doumanas and males. Our hope is that such a council will find a way to end this confusion before a crisis arrives."

Jonton nodded. "Yes. We have identified the same problems. But a council is not the answer. A council is too many voices, each with her," Jonton's eyebrow ridges rose slightly, "or *his* own needs and desires. Kler doumanas want what's best for the kler. Commune doumanas want what's best for their particular commune." She glanced at Azlii, but made no mention of what corentans might want. "A council sounds good, noble even, but it simply won't work."

The greenish-orange of amazement and the red-purple of amusement blushed lightly on Azlii's neck. Only a corentan, I thought, would be amused at such a pointed slight.

"Seems to me," Azlii said, "that you can't know what will or won't work without trying it. You're an orindle. Your life is dedicated to experimentation, to discovering the truth through testing. It's not very orindle-like to make a pronouncement that's nothing more than a guess."

Jonton glared at Azlii. "The corentan reputation for plain speech is well-deserved, I see."

Azlii's smile was both amused and cold. "Oh, corentans can talk pretty when we want to. This just doesn't seem like the moment." She leaned forward.

"The situation is serious. A solution has to be found quickly or we're all—kler, commune, and corenta—going to find ourselves with bigger problems than heavy rain and a planet that has taken to sudden shaking."

"Yes," Jonton said, carefully setting her cup on the low table. "And we have found that solution. Not based on a guess, but on well-reasoned ideas and local testing. We gave Larta a try, put her in charge of all of Chimbalay, only to discover she lacked a hand strong enough to hold the guide stick."

Larta's neck erupted in a mass of brown-black spots—likely both at the idea that the orindles had *put* her in charge, and the accusation that she hadn't done her job well—but her face stayed calm.

"There is only one group strong enough to set our world back on the right path," Jonton said, "and that is the orindles. For exactly the reasons you said, Azlii."

She rolled Azlii's name so that it sounded like a hiss. The dark-yellow-green of surprise lit on two of Larta's spots. I was sure she purposely hadn't mentioned Azlii's name. No colors showed on Jonton's throat—she was a trained orindle, after all—but my lumani eyes saw how the orange-red of anticipation and the dark-gray-purple of frustration swirled through her.

"Because," Jonton said, "only orindles are trained to observe and experiment and choose the best practices. Without us in charge, chaos will destroy our world." Her voice softened. "We hope, very much hope, that you see the wisdom of this and will join us as Seconds, helping to have our orders fulfilled."

"That doesn't seem the best use of any guardian's

time," Larta said evenly. No spots were lit on her neck now.

Jonton means you, too, I sent to Azlii. *For you to get Kelroosh and the other corentas to take the orindle's orders.*

Unlikely, Azlii sent back.

Jonton shrugged. She nodded to her helper, who stepped forward and refilled our cups. Jonton and my sisters lifted their cups and drank. I took a tiny sip, to stay in harmony with Azlii, Larta, and Nez.

"That's quite sad and unfortunate," Jonton said, setting her cup back on the table. "I had hoped you would see that not only is our scheme the best way, it is the only way. You will stay as our guests, so we can discuss this further."

"That's not possible," Larta said. "We all have work to do."

She pulled herself to her feet, wavered, and then collapsed.

Thirteen

I jumped up from the long chair and sank down on my heels next to Larta, my fingers moving softly but quickly over her emotion spots. They were warm, but not right somehow. Nez moaned, and then collapsed on the floor beside the guardian. My gaze shot up to Azlii. She pulled her spine straight a moment, her eyes wide, and put a hand to her head before falling off the long chair and thudding on the floor. I glanced at Jonton, who hadn't moved from her seat, her muck-colored eyes focused on me, her hands folded in her lap.

Drugged. It must have been in the drink, and hadn't affected me because I'd had only the tiniest swallow. Jonton, too, must have sipped. I remembered now how the rim of the cup had barely touched her mouth. Jonton kept her eyes on me, her head tilting slightly as if in an unasked question: why hadn't I fallen over, too? I mimicked Azlii, widening my eyes and putting my hands to my head before shutting my eyes and falling over next to my sisters.

"You know where to take them," Jonton said.

I kept my eyes closed and heard the soft scrape of feet moving, wheels rolling across the redstone floor, and low grunts. The sound of something being dropped and landing hard. The low, hollow ring of struck metal. Rough hands grabbed me under my armpits and held my feet, lifted me into the air and swung my body slightly upwards—then a small fall, and the feel of something cold and hard beneath my back. The sound of wheels again, and the sense of movement. Then a soft whoosh that I thought must be the door irising opening.

I let my head loll to the side and took a chance, cracking open my eyes just wide enough to see, and glimpsed Nez's hand, her limp arm draped over the side of a rolling cart, and a wall painted the pale-yellow-blue of acceptance. We came to a stop. Another door irised open. First Nez, then Azlii, and finally Larta were wheeled past, through the opened door. I closed my eyes again, in fear that someone would see me looking.

"Where does she go?" a voice near my feet said.

"To Hope," a different voice answered. "Research Center Three. Through the passageway, not the street."

I felt the cart I lay on back up slightly and then turn, as I was wheeled in a different direction than my sisters had been taken. We came to what must have been a ramp; I could feel that we were going down. At the bottom of the ramp, the helphand grunted as she turned the cart and started in a new direction.

I hazarded another look, barely slitting open my eyes. The hallway seemed long. Light globes glowed overhead, which meant we were probably below street level. The walls and ceiling were painted orange-red. I wanted to turn my head, get a better look at where we were, but I couldn't chance it. I closed my eyes again.

We continued down the long, flat hall, and then must have come to another ramp. The helphand began breathing hard. I guessed we were going up—likely as far up as we'd come down. There was a whoosh, and I felt a slight bump. We came to a stop. I wanted to look, but was afraid to until I heard steps leading away, and then another whoosh. I braved a quick glance that showed me the door was closing.

"It's all right, Khe. You can stop pretending now."

I knew Pradat's voice. I trusted she wouldn't have said that unless it was true.

I opened my eyes and sat up.

"I don't understand," I said, my gaze darting around the small room, the walls painted greenish-blue, the color of hope, and no one in it but Pradat and me.

Before she could answer, the door irised open again and Jonton walked in.

"Good," Jonton said to Pradat, "you've brought her out of it quickly. She's different from the others, isn't she?"

Pradat shrugged. "The lumani changed her, but we don't know exactly how or how much."

"Her emotion spots don't light," Jonton said, "or at least, didn't during our meeting. Maybe she has no emotions left. Or doesn't really care about things she claims to." She dusted her hands against her thighs. "Well, that may be something to explore in later days. For now—" she bent slightly to bring her face near to mine, "—how are you feeling, Khe?"

"A bit dazed," I said honestly. "I don't understand why you've done this?"

"To talk to you alone. I have a feeling about you. I think, had things been different, you would have made a fine orindle. You like to know things, don't you? The how and why of it? The way things work?"

"Most doumanas want to know that," I said.

"Yes, some do. But not with the same burn and desire you feel." She leaned over and took my left arm, turning it so the dots on my wrist showed plainly. "You're running out of time. Commemoration Day will be here soon, but unfortunately, you won't. Unless…"

"Jonton knows about the treatments," Pradat said.

It seemed Jonton knew about a lot of things.

"Pradat is brilliant," she said. "I've no doubt that the treatments she's devised will save you. Sadly, Pradat's work here is so important that she will no longer be allowed to treat you in the corenta. You would have to be here, in Chimbalay, an easy thing to arrange. You could stay with Larta in Justice House, as you have been since you arrived. Pradat would continue the treatments. You would live a long, cheerful life."

"And in return?"

Jonton shrugged. "You have influence over Larta and Azlii. I know you can help them see the obvious truth of why the orindles should be in charge, not only in Chimbalay, but throughout our world."

"Larta and Azlii aren't easily swayed." I couldn't shake the feeling that Jonton wanted more than she said.

The orindle shifted her dark eyes to Pradat. "You haven't brought your equipment? Khe needs another treatment today or she'll slip back from the good you've done her."

"I have everything set up in another room," Pradat

said.

Jonton turned back to me. "Pradat truly is brilliant. It would be a shame for her to fail to help persuade you on this matter. That's part of her work, too—persuasion. And if she fails... shunning is such an unpleasant fate."

I held my breath, thinking Jonton was little different from the lumani—from Weast—both promising me life in return for doing what they desired. At least Weast never threatened one of my sisters with shunning if I didn't do its bidding.

"Where are my sisters? Are they well?"

"Quite well. Here, in the research center, recovering from their sudden sleep. They'll be on their way soon."

"That's good. I'm sure as soon as they are recovered you will send them back to Justice House."

I looked at the dots on my wrist and swallowed hard. Everything came down to time—minutes, hours, and days—to learn the orindle's weaknesses, to devise a plan, to live. "I suppose Pradat and I should get on with the treatments."

-=o=-

The moment Jonton left, Pradat touched her finger to my lips, in sign we shouldn't speak. Her warning wasn't needed—I'd already reasoned that no spoken words were safe from being overheard in this place—but it was good to know that she was aware and worried too. It was another sign that she and I were still on the same side.

Azlii, I sent, as Pradat and I walked toward the treatment room.

No reply.

Azlii. Can you hear me?

Still silence.

And then, a small sound, like many birds calling and squawking at once. I couldn't catch what direction the sound came from—it seemed to exist only in my earholes. I scrubbed at them with the palms of my hands.

Khe, I heard softly inside my head—Azlii's voice.

Where are you? I sent. But no response came back.

Azlii, I sent again, watching the thought grains hang in the air a moment before they disappeared beyond the hallway wall. Still no answer.

"Turn here," Pradat said when we came to a split in the hallway. "The treatment room is just there." She pointed to a door painted the pink of nurturing.

We're at the treatment room, I sent, hoping Azlii could hear me, even if I couldn't hear her.

The pink door irised open as we neared it. I didn't know if Pradat had done something to activate it, or if there was some kind of eye that saw us coming.

My mind was spinning with worries for Nez, Azlii, and Larta. Jonton said they were awake and well, but I didn't trust most of what Jonton said. Still, maybe they had left Research Center Three and were too far away for my thoughts to reach. I didn't know how far away think-talk could be heard. Azlii could send all the way from Chimbalay's center to Kelroosh on the plain beyond the gates, but my ability didn't seem to be as strong as hers.

The equipment in the treatment room was much like what she'd brought to Kelroosh, plus a few things

149

more. The chair here was raised high off the ground and had a sort of hard pillow above the back for my head to rest against. I wished the chair were lower. I always felt better with my feet on the ground.

Pradat had her back to me, bent over a table, busy with her preparations. There was one window in the room and I turned my head to look out. The day was still dark outside. A soft rain was falling.

Azlii! I sent, and received only silence for my efforts.

Pradat looked over her shoulder at me. "Nervous?"

I drummed my fingers on my thigh. "My sisters must be nearly back at Justice House by now, don't you think?"

"Perhaps," Pradat said. "Though Jonton may have decided to offer them hospitality here, despite what she told you, the better to convince them of the wisdom of her plan."

"I thought that was my task."

"It's the task of every doumana to do what is best for her sisters," Pradat said as she walked over to where I was seated. She lifted my arm, peered at my age spots and frowned. "I had hoped they would have at least begun to fade, if not to disappear."

My neck felt hot. "The treatments aren't working?"

Pradat shrugged. "How have you been feeling? Still tired?"

"Not as much as I was. Not since the last treatment."

"Something is working then," Pradat said as she fixed a tube under my skin. "This is a different infusion. You know I've been working with the babblers—not that *you* are a babbler, Khe, nor that I see any danger of you becoming one—but we are learning a lot from them. A side effect of a new treatment has been an increase in their energy fields. We don't know what that will mean in the long run, but for you we want the opposite. The lumani sped your natural energy. I want to slow it. This infusion is the antidote to the mild poison speeding the energy of the babblers."

I listened but it didn't matter to me what technique she was trying. My thoughts were on Azlii, Larta, and Nez. And Marnka, who'd saved my life in the wilderness.

I looked up at Pradat. "Is Marnka among the babblers you're treating?"

Pradat pressed her lips together. "No. If she is still alive, she's likely in the wilderness."

I heard the bird noises in my earholes again. A tremble raced across my shoulders. Why was I hearing things?

Pradat peered into my eyes. "What's wrong?"

I licked my lips. "Nothing. Just worried about the treatments. If they'll work." I swallowed hard. "I wonder how they will change me. Change me more, I mean. I'm already different."

"You don't seem different to me," Pradat said in that noncommittal voice that made me want to scream. "Not in the core."

"But I am," I said. "You said yourself my energy field is sped up. Things are happening to me. I hear sounds that aren't there. I see things my sisters don't. My spots don't light any more. If I'm not a doumana, what am I?"

"You are Khe. Why do you need to be anything else?"

Because all I ever wanted was to be like my sisters. I had new sisters now, but I wasn't like them any more than I was like the doumanas at Lunge.

The birdcalls sounded again, louder this time. I put my hands over my earholes, trying to make it stop.

I heard Azlii's voice in my head, think-talking to me. *We're on the move. Me, Larta, and Nez. I don't know where the orindles are taking us. They said to the door, but this walk is too long to be leading outside. We seem to be going* down. *Maybe to lower rooms?*

Can you get away from the orindles? I sent. *Find your own way out?*

There are too many of them.

I wanted to ask Pradat if she knew about rooms below ground, but I was afraid to speak. The walls seem to know how to listen and repeat in this place, and I'd already said too much.

The door irised open and Jonton, accompanied by two helphands in yellow hipwraps, strode in.

FOURTEEN

"Have you finished with her?" Jonton asked Pradat.

Jonton stood not even a hand's breadth away and yet, for her, I was barely there, no more important than a beaker simmering above a flame. But *Khe*—the idea of me—that mattered to her.

The brown-yellow of annoyance showed on two of Pradat's spots. Purposely, it must have been, since Pradat was adept at hiding her emotions. Now it suited her to let them show.

Jonton put a smile on her lips. "These things can't be rushed, can they? Take the time you need."

"You may want to wait outside," Pradat said. "It will be a while still."

"I'd like to observe," Jonton said. "I so rarely get to see you at your work. And certainly it will be educational for the helphands."

I glanced at the two yellow-clad helphands who stood on either side of the door, like sentries. Their gazes flicked between Jonton and me. A shiver of nerves shot up my breastbone. I didn't want to be on display.

"Not much to see," Pradat said, fiddling with some dials and then consulting the instrument she wore strapped to her palm.

"Nevertheless," Jonton said, "we will remain."

Frustration rumbled through me that I couldn't think-talk to Pradat. She had something going on in her mind—I was sure of that—but I had no way to ask her. All I could do was sit quietly while fluids pumped into my body and pinpointed lights heated the back of my neck and a tiny spot low on my forehead. I wanted to jump off the chair. I needed my feet on the floor at least.

Pradat had slowed her movements, was taking a very long time to consult her instruments and record the results. The brown-purple of exasperation showed briefly on Jonton's neck, a flash so minute that had I not been looking at the exact moment I wouldn't have seen it. I wanted Pradat to hurry, too. Jonton would take me to Nez, Azlii, and Larta—I felt sure of that. I wanted to be with my sisters. I needed to know they were safe.

Pradat seemed to have run out of stalling tactics. She slowly flipped the switch on first one and then another of the light-focusing machines, turning them off. She consulted her palm instrument again, before she began removing the tubes from my arms.

"I'll need to see her tomorrow," Pradat told Jonton. "At this point in the treatment, a follow-up is critical."

"Of course." Jonton nodded to the helphands at the door, then turned her attention to me. "I trust you appreciate all that Pradat has done and is doing for you." She let that sink in a moment, her eyes boring into mine, then put her hand lightly on my elbow. "You must be anxious to talk to your companions. We'll take you to them."

The two helphands fell in beside me as soon as the

door shut behind us. Jonton and Pradat walked ahead. I saw Pradat's unhappiness—the colors swirling through her—though I wasn't sure what caused this emotion. Nothing showed on Pradat's neck, any more than the excitement I saw in Jonton showed on hers. The helphands, though, were about as private in their feelings as hatchlings. The bright-blue of excitement glowed on their skins.

What would my neck show if my spots still lit? I wondered. Nerves. Anticipation. Curiosity. Anger. My neck would display more colors than the sky during Resonance, when the air shimmered with the hues we followed to our mating grounds.

We traveled a long, white hallway—white floor, white walls, white ceiling—the color of satisfaction, another emotion I saw swirling in Jonton. Her ease made me all the more anxious.

At the end of the hallway a door, blending so well with the wall that I didn't spot it, irised open with an almost silent whoosh. A set of stairs lay behind it.

Azlii, I sent. *They're bringing me below ground. Where are you now?*

An empty room, she sent back. *Not so empty, actually. There's the three of us and six helphands, each with her neck glowing orange-red.*

Orange-red. Anticipation. Jonton had a surprise planned. A surprise everyone knew about except Azlii, Larta, Nez, and me. I couldn't tell if Pradat was unhappy because she knew what was coming, or because she didn't. I didn't know if the faint thumping I heard coming from beneath our feet had anything to do with the helphands' excitement.

155

At the bottom of the stairs another well-hidden door irised open to reveal another hallway. Greenish-blue, the walls and floor of this one—the color of amazement—and freshly painted. This building may have been built to lumani specifications, but the paint was doumana-chosen. The lumani hadn't seen colors the way we did, and they didn't understand the colors emotions sparked. Why would doumanas want this underground place to evoke amazement?

Another door opened and my sisters were ushered into the hallway with us. I wanted to run to them and stroke their necks. I could see the same urge in them, but the helphands nudged themselves between each of us, keeping us apart while we followed Jonton forward. The faint thumping sound grew louder.

And then I knew why greenish-blue had been chosen. Behind the last door, in an all-white room, was an incredible machine—twice my height and so wide that if I held hands with my three sisters and we stretched out our arms we would not cover its face. Dials and levers on a panel nearly as big as I was glowed in the darkened room. I heard Pradat gasp, and saw that this room was as much of a surprise to her as it was to me.

"We found this after the lumani were destroyed." Jonton's outline gleamed with the bright-green of pride. "At first, no doumana would admit to knowing what the machine did, or how to work it, but of course there had to be those who knew. The lumani were clever, but without hands they couldn't control any machines themselves. They had to have help. First to build it, and then to make it work. Eventually we found them here, a sisterhood so secret that once they'd entered this structure, they never left it again and were shown on the rolls as Returned."

"What is it?" Nez asked.

Jonton grinned. "Something amazing. Did you never wonder why our planet was blessed with seasons that came at exactly the same time each year, with perfect weather for the crops that grew in each region? Every year, the perfect amount of rain, at the right time, the perfect amount of sun." She swept her arm toward the machine. "This is why."

Azlii stepped forward and stretched one hand toward the machine, her fingers stopping just shy of it. She waved her hand back and forth, as though the machine could be read through the still air between it and her fingertips.

"A weather machine," she said.

"Very good." Jonton clapped one hand against her thigh. "Developed after a disaster with the weather-prophets."

Disaster was the right word—a failed try at breeding weather-prophets that only succeeded in making babblers, like Marnka.

"It must have been quickly and recently done," I said. "The *disaster* only happened ten or twelve years ago. Every year since then our weather has remained the same."

Jonton sent me a sharp look. This was information I shouldn't have, and I was foolish to have let it fly from my mouth. Thinking of Marnka had made me angry over what had been done to her. Had made me remember what she'd told me about the true history of the weather-prophets.

Jonton's gaze dropped to my neck. My spots should have been lit, and she seemed pleased that they weren't. Her own neck was again lit with three dark-red-blue spots of curiosity—colors she must have allowed to show. I was going to have to watch my words more carefully.

Jonton's eyebrow ridges rose, then relaxed. "It was quickly but well done. The doumanas who tended the machine for the lumani had little to do other than make sure things kept running as they were meant to."

"Pftt," Azlii said. "They must not have done a good job, given all the unseasonal rain we're receiving."

"They did a fine job." Jonton reached up and stroked a dial as though it were a sister. "The lumani were clever, but we orindles are cleverer. After the lumani were gone it was *we* who reasoned out how the machine worked. We who brought the rain." Her gaze cut across each of us, one by one. "This is why the orindles of Chimbalay must be in charge of rebuilding our world. None other have the intelligence and the resources."

"You'd better stop the rain now in that case, before the ground is too wet for planting." Azlii leaned slightly toward Jonton. "You do understand that wet soil will rot the seeds."

"I would have expected that comment from a commune doumana like Khe," Jonton said. "I'm quite surprised a *corentan* knows so much about crop growing."

"Corentans know quite a bit about many things," Azlii said.

"How does it work?" My voice was small, but the spike of curiosity was huge in me. I was desperate to understand. It was a lumani desperation, a *need* for knowledge, like a need for air.

Jonton lifted her hand again to the dial. "Let me show you." She pressed a dial, and turned her back. All we could see were her elbows and upper arms moving as she did whatever she was doing. She turned to face us and swept her arm toward a long clear reservoir built beside the wall closest to where Nez stood. The machine whirred softly. I caught a whiff of a scent in the air that I couldn't place, something unpleasantly sharp.

The reservoir began to lightly cloud as a few drops of moisture fell into it.

"It's raining outside now," Jonton said.

Larta laughed low. "It was raining yesterday, raining this morning, raining when we arrived. Why should now be different?"

Jonton nodded. "But not like this." She turned her back to us again, moving more levers and dials, I supposed. I leaned to the side and lifted to my toes, trying to see over Jonton's shoulders to what she was doing, but she hid her movements too well. I sidestepped to get a better view. One of the helphands grabbed my upper arm and pulled me back.

Water began flowing into the tall reservoir, at first just a couple of finger widths at the bottom, but then like into a bucket when the tap is turned wide. A hand's-breadth of water. Half an arm's worth. Fingers to shoulders. Foot to waist. Water that had pinged in at first now tumbled into the reservoir.

The room seemed tinged dark-gray, but the lights were bright above and around us. It was my sisters' worry I was seeing on their necks, in the air. Jonton turned, and her throat was washed bright-green with pride and white with satisfaction. Her happiness angered me. Hers wasn't the sort of happiness that would have turned her neck crimson, but a different sort of joy, something without a name or a color. Something too ugly to deserve a name or color. Something smug and ambitious that didn't belong in any doumana.

Her lips crinkled and she fiddled with the dials and levers again. The water filling the reservoir began to slow. Finally it topped off at a spot above my head. The reservoir was as big around as I was. I tried to gauge how deep that much water falling on flat land would measure. I couldn't figure it exactly. I didn't have that sort of mind. But I knew enough to guess that when we walked out of here to return to Justice House the puddles would be deep.

"Remember what you've seen here today," Jonton said. "Tell your sisters what the orindles can do."

"What you can do," I said.

Jonton smiled.

She looked toward the helphand closest to the door, then turned back and began to work the dials and levers again. She could be turning down the rain to let us walk back dry, or turning it up, to make sure her lesson struck home with us. I couldn't guess which.

I glanced around the room, wondering where the low moan I heard came from. A low rumble followed the moan. Nez caught my eye and two spots lit with the dark-red-blue of curiosity. I touched my ear hole, wondering if she heard the sounds too, but she raised her eyebrow ridges and shrugged.

A louder rumble caught everyone's attention, but it passed quickly.

The helphand waved her hand over a small indentation on the wall. As the door began to iris open, the floor beneath our feet buckled. The helphand at the door cried out. A piece of the ceiling, as big as a hatchling's head, crashed near my feet. Larta grabbed my arm and we tumbled to the ground together.

Fifteen

Jonton wobbled and stumbled the few steps to me, the ground still shivering lightly beneath us. She closed her hand around my wrist and pulled me to my feet. Larta sat up and rubbed her leg where a chunk of fallen ceiling had hit her. A couple of helphands bustled Nez and Azlii out of the room. I pulled free of Jonton's grip and crouched next to Larta. She'd tugged off her hipwrap and was using it to mop up the blood leaking from the gash on her leg.

"Are you badly hurt?"

Larta's neck showed the gray-green of disgust. At herself, I guessed, that she, the First of the guardians, charged with protecting the doumanas of Chimbalay, was the only one injured.

She wadded up the soiled hipwrap. "I'm fine. Now help me up."

I stood and held my hand out. Larta gripped it and helped herself up, using me as a counterweight. When she let go I slipped and knocked against the machine. I heard a loud whoosh, like steam escaping, and smelled, oddly, the same, sharp ozone scent of Weast. I jumped away, though the machine didn't feel hot to the touch.

Jonton grabbed my arm and tugged me further from the machine.

"What?" Larta asked.

"This room's integrity might be compromised," Jonton said. "The structure technicians will say when we can come in here again." She pushed me toward the door, but not hard. "We need to get you out of here, Khe, before more ceiling falls."

Why was she so anxious to get *me* out? Shouldn't she have said 'you both out' or 'we all need to get out'? But it was my name she used, and me she nudged toward the door.

Larta caught it too. "Do go. I'll hobble on behind as best I can on my own."

Jonton gave her a hard look but called to one of the helphands to come to Larta's aid.

Outside the room, technicians had arrived and were already examining fresh cracks in the greenish-blue walls of the hall. As soon as we were out, three techs in black hipwraps picked up the kits they'd set on the floor and hurried into the room. The door irised closed behind them.

"We'll return to the receiving room to talk further," Jonton said, and sidled past the techs, helphands, Nez, and Azlii who stood between her and the stairwell.

Back in the receiving room, Jonton didn't invite us to sit or offer refreshments. She herded Azlii, Larta, Nez, Pradat and me together, and dismissed her helphands.

"You've heard what I have to say." Her voice was quiet and calm, her eyes focused on me alone. "You have seen what we can do. *Some* of what we can do. There's more. Much more. In time, once the orindles have moved to a position of bringing order, we will show you other wonders, things that will amaze and

163

please you. We'll meet again in the morning, after Khe's treatment."

"Larta needs treatment now," Pradat said. "I'll see to her wound before these doumanas leave."

"Of course," Jonton said, and looked at Larta as if only now realizing she was hurt. "You will all stay here at the research center tonight. The streets are wet. The night is cold."

Two spots on Nez's neck showed the blue-red of anxiety. Larta didn't seem to like the idea much either.

"A quick stick job will take care of Larta's injury," Pradat said.

"And then we'll be on our way," Larta said.

Jonton nodded. "As you wish." She looked at me again for a long moment, then clapped Pradat's shoulder. "I leave them in your care. I know you will do what's best."

"First off, Larta needs to sit and stretch out her leg," Pradat said, and pointed to the chair she wanted her to take.

Jonton nodded. "Whatever needs to be done." She turned and glided away, her feet barely lifting from the floor as she made her way out.

The feeling in the room changed the instant Jonton left. Azlii exhaled, and her hitched up shoulders came down a finger's width. No one spoke while Pradat fixed Larta's leg, pinching the wound shut and sticking the ragged skin back together with a yellow plaster she cured with a small green light.

The hard storm had passed, leaving a soft drizzle behind, but the streets were slick with water. Our progress was slow, made slower by Larta's injury. The tall obelisks that provided light gleamed bright-pink in their watery coats. The rain had pooled in low spots. We had to watch where we stepped or find ourselves plunged into water halfway to our knees.

Even on the street we didn't feel safe to talk. Doumanas were about, wrapped up tight in warm, unseasonable Barren Season cloaks, grumbling among themselves about the rain. Any one of them could be a spy.

Azlii pitched her voice to a whisper. "We should go to Kelroosh."

It was a long, wet walk to the gate, and then a cold, wet walk across the plain. Azlii's comment was the last thing said among us until we were safely inside Kelroosh's walls. Home threw open the door before we'd even reached the far corner of our structure, as glad to see us, I thought, as we were to see it. And thoughtful, having warmed the room.

Everyone but Nez sat and pulled off our foot casings. Nez paced the room, her wet casings still on her feet.

"Orindles," she said, her spots blazing brown-black with anger and gray-green with disgust.

Larta raised her eyebrow ridges. "Good thing Pradat stayed in Chimbalay."

"I'll make something warm for us to drink," Azlii said, and headed toward the little communiteria off the receiving room. I looked at her neck to see what she was feeling, but the only color there was the ocher of impatience. For all that we could see how our sisters felt, we couldn't guess at what was in their minds or hearts—what caused the emotions.

"Pradat's only half an orindle, as far as I'm concerned," Nez said. "She's kind. Besides, she's helping Khe."

"And why do we think that is?" Larta asked. "Did you notice how, when the world shook, the only one Jonton worried about was Khe?" She looked at me. "Remember, Pradat and Jonton are sister-orindles."

"Pradat came to warn us that the orindles wanted control," Nez said. "She wouldn't do that if she were fully in harmony with Jonton."

"She's not," I said quietly. Pradat had put herself at risk to save me from the lumani. There was nothing false about her.

Larta hiked up one shoulder in a partial shrug. "Maybe so."

Azlii returned, pushing a rolling cart containing a steaming pot and four cups.

"It's always about Khe, though," Larta said. "First Simanca, then the lumani, now Jonton. Everyone wants her for themselves."

Nez reached over and stroked my throat. "It's not Khe's fault. She never asked for any of this."

Except that I had. I'd wanted the original surgery to restore my ability to feel Resonance. I'd enjoyed—reveled in—my ability to push the crops. I'd asked—demanded—the chance to live my own life, under my own control. And what had it led to? The destruction of the lumani, harm to Chimbalay, and maybe harm to our entire world. All because I wanted to mate. Because I wanted to be normal.

Azlii poured a red liquid from the pot into the first of the four cups. "Warm zwas. I figured we could use a cup or two to shake off the cold, and Jonton."

I wasn't sure something intoxicating was the best thing at this moment, but I took the cup when she handed it to me.

Nez cradled her cup between her hands. "If the rain doesn't stop, what will happen?"

"We'll starve," I said. "None of our crops can take that much water and thrive. The lumani tricked us. By engineering a perfect world, they engineered our end when that perfect world went away."

"Pftt." Azlii handed the last cup to Larta, took her own, and settled onto a floor pillow. "It's Jonton who's destroying our world, not the lumani. It's Jonton who has to be stopped."

Larta's lips turned in the slightest of smiles. "No thought to giving the orindles what they want?"

Azlii hiked up one shoulder in a shrug. "Doesn't affect us corentans one way or the other, no more than the lumani did. What about you, guardian? Do you look forward to being Second under the orindles' rule?"

"I look forward to again serving superior minds," Larta said, and grinned.

A sudden chill rolled through me. "Commune structures. They aren't built like structures in a corenta or a kler. They aren't made to withstand this kind of weather. If it keeps raining, they'll dissolve. Commune doumanas won't have food or shelter."

Home sent, *Thank you for thinking of the structures, Khe. We seem to be forgotten in your conversations. Corentan structures are strong, but even we will crumble if enough water falls on us.*

Azlii's hand was at her mouth, holding the cup she was about to empty down her throat. She sent her gaze my way. She'd obviously heard what Home had sent, but finished her drink before setting the cup beside her on the floor. "Then we must stop the rain."

Nez nodded. "But how?"

"Not by blowing up a part of Chimbalay again," Azlii said. "Someone is going to have to convince Jonton to give up her dream." She looked at Larta. "Or maybe the guardians can help. Can't you just seize her and hold her someplace?"

Larta scratched a spot near her earhole. "Stopping Jonton won't stop the rain. Not if she has the machine already programmed. We don't know that she's the only one who can work it, either. She said there were doumanas helping the lumani. They would know how. She could have trained any number of her orindle-sisters."

"If we could find the ones who helped the lumani," Nez said, "they could stop it."

My throat felt scratchy. I stood and walked toward the rolling cart and the last of the zwas, cold in its pot now from sitting. "We'd have to get into Research Center Three. Jonton said the doumanas who served the lumani never left once they entered, which likely means some are still there. Jonton could have moved them out, but that would be the place to start."

"I doubt Jonton is going to let anyone wander around inside, tapping on doors, to find them," Azlii said.

I shrugged and filled my cup. "Maybe Pradat could. I think Jonton still trusts her."

"Even if we could find one," Larta said, "she'd have to be willing to help. And Jonton would have to be confined—all of the orindles, since we don't know which would fight to carry out Jonton's plan. And every helphand. It would be impossible. Plus, we need the orindles and helphands. Doumanas get sick, they become injured— someone has to care for them."

Hard, fat raindrops pinged against the windows. Four heads turned to look as the water sluiced down the pane.

"We have to destroy the machine," I said.

Larta turned her gaze back to me. "We'd have to figure out how to destroy it first. And then, same problem: we'd have to get into the research center. We'd have to get to the machine."

Slowly, slowly, Nez shifted around to look at us. "I think I know how to destroy it."

Sixteen

The room was quiet. Even Home held its breath, I think.

Nez hunched slightly into her shoulders. "Water. The machine must use electricity. All the water that's filling the streets—we route it into the machine room and drown it. It'll go down in a giant sizzle."

Larta drummed her fingers on her thigh. "That'd be quite an undertaking. We'd have to find a pool of water deep enough and figure out how to transport the water to the research center, how to siphon it down into the room. The room is below ground. There aren't any windows."

"But it could work," Nez said, the greenish-blue of hope firing into color on her neck.

"It could work," Larta said. "But the logistics. I don't know how we'd get it done without being seen and stopped."

I sat up very straight. "Maybe we could turn the machine on itself. Did you notice that when the rain was falling at its hardest, that's when the planet shook? I think maybe the machine is causing it. If that's so, we could make the rain fall so hard that the machine collapses the room around itself."

"How would we make the machine work?" Azlii asked. "We don't know how. We'd have to make

Jonton do it, and I doubt she's going to help us."

Kroot kroot, Home sent, wanting our attention.

Do you have an idea, Home? Azlii sent.

Sadly, no. Pradat is coming. Walking very fast through Kelroosh.

Azlii pulled herself to her feet. "I'll warm some more zwas. I think we're going to need it."

-=o=-

No color showed on Pradat's neck to tell us what she was feeling as she rushed into the receiving room, swept off her wet cloak and removed her sodden, muddy foot casings. I wondered what it had cost her to hide her emotions like that. She had no need to hide them from us, yet I think the habit was so strong in her that to let her spots light took conscious effort.

"You have news," Azlii said, pouring a cup of zwas for Pradat.

Plain-necked or not, Pradat wouldn't have rushed here without news.

She took the cup and swallowed down a deep drink. "I'm not sure where to begin."

"The beginning is usually a good spot," Azlii said.

Pradat laughed under her breath, poured a swallow or two more of zwas into her cup and downed them. She placed the cup back on the rolling cart and finally settled onto an empty pillow next to Larta.

"I've been told something. I'm not sure what to make of it." Pradat ran a hand over her scalp. "We all saw how Jonton rushed to protect Khe when the planet shivered."

"Trah," Larta said, and waved one hand as if

171

flicking Jonton away from her. "I could have lain on the floor bleeding until next Barren Season and she wouldn't have noticed. All her concern was for Khe."

Pradat raised her eyebrow ridges in agreement. "She knows Khe is back in Kelroosh. I think she's afraid the corenta will leave and she'll lose Khe forever. Jonton has asked that Khe come again to Chimbalay. Alone. She says if Khe does, and listens to what she has to say, she will stop the rain."

-=o=-

The room was warm, flames crackling and popping in the firecave near where I sat, the smell of burning wood pleasant. I kept my feet together, my eyes cast down the way I would when called to Simanca's dwelling in the old days at Lunge—but now it was a way to observe without seeming to.

Pradat stood just inside the door chatting with the two orindles and a helphand who'd escorted us to the room. I didn't know why we needed three doumanas to escort us two, and I didn't think the casual sound of Pradat's conversation with her sisters was the whole truth. No spots lit on any of the well-trained orindles' necks. The helphand showed only the slightest trace of purple-gray concern. Concern for what? At Lunge, with sisters I'd lived with all my life, whose experiences were nearly identical to mine, any of us could see that color and know its cause immediately. But not here, not among strangers who saw through eyes educated by different experiences, minds filled with other ways of thinking.

Rain fell outside, steady rivulets running down the

outside of the windows—rain that had begun only moments after Pradat and I had entered the research center.

The door irised open and Jonton came in. The three escorts left the room, leaving Pradat alone by the jambs. Jonton nodded as she passed Pradat and walked quickly across the room to where I sat. She reached out a hand and I feared for a moment she was going to stroke my neck as though we felt warmly toward each other, but she swept into the chair next to mine without our skins touching. The door shut with a whispered whoosh.

"I'm pleased you've come, Khe." She smiled, and her eyes flickered to my throat and mouth, waiting. I didn't give the return smile or warm emotion colors she clearly wanted. She closed her own smile down and said, "You are a very interesting doumana, but you already know that. You know you are different—have been different from the beginning. But not static. Not unchanging. Oh, no." She tilted her head. "Do you know what possible clay is?"

"No," I said.

"It's dug from the banks of only one river, a long way from here. The clay is naturally black but can be stained any shade. The black doesn't dim the color—it enhances it, makes it shine. Its particles are fine, smooth and densely loaded, very strong. Almost anything can be made of it. Whatever size or shape or color thing you dream up, with this clay, it's possible to create it."

"Oh," I said, not seeing the connection.

Jonton leaned forward and patted my knee. "I was

close to the Powers, you know. One of the few privileged to receive direct communication from them, to know their secrets. I know what was done in the special room in Research Center One."

I held very still and listened.

"You are the possible clay," Jonton said. "You were infertile, but we orindles changed your shape and you laid your egg. You were angry, and you changed your own shape and ran off to Chimbalay. The Powers found you—the lumani—and they changed your shape again to suit their own purposes."

My neck flamed. No one knew what had happened in that room—no one but Weast and the other lumani, and me. If Jonton knew, really knew how Weast had used its machine to form its dreadful egg in me, how could I bear that shame? I glared at her, glad that she couldn't see on my throat the anger and disgust I felt.

"The question now, Khe, is what shape you will take finally. In the end, you are the shape of our future—but what will you be? What will we be? That question must be answered."

I wanted to say that she was wrong, that I was Khe, just as I'd always been, but that wasn't true.

Jonton turned up her palms. "Pradat and I don't have exact harmony of feelings about you. She wants to prolong your life and send you off to do whatever little things you might with your time. But, Khe—look at you. You've already developed the ability to see far distances and have superior hearing—yes, we know about these. You rarely eat or sleep." She smiled kindly. "Don't be angry at Pradat. She is quite observant, and it's her duty to report all her findings."

I knew all about duty; Simanca had been brilliant at using our natural sense of it to get what she wanted. I wasn't angry with Pradat. I understood her.

Jonton leaned toward me. "Think what can be accomplished without those needs. I believe you will develop a heightened mind as well. Like the lumani, you will see what needs to be done and the way to do it. Think what that will mean when all of us are like you—the solutions we will find in a fraction of the time it takes now."

Color had begun to show on her throat as she spoke, the bright-blue of excitement and the greenish-blue of hope.

"Think on this, too," Jonton said. "Only you can give this gift to all your sisters and brothers. It is the perfect atonement for what you did in Chimbalay."

I thought of Marnka and the other weather-prophets the lumani and orindles had tried to 'improve.' They'd become babblers, their minds, and ultimately their lives, lost. Was Jonton one of the orindles who'd helped the lumani in those experiments?

I glanced at Pradat. She'd been silent while Jonton spoke. I'd seen into her, though, the ambivalence she felt—wanting to spare me from Jonton, but wanting to know the same things Jonton was curious about.

I thought quickly, wondering how much I could wring from Jonton's greed to have me.

"I'd like to know the answers to your question as much as you do. I'll stay and help and do my best on two conditions. One, Pradat will be allowed to finish her treatments."

"Of course," Jonton said. "We want you healthy, to become what you will become. Resonance is next year. We want you to be here to feel it, and go to your nesting site, mate, and lay your egg as is the right and duty of every doumana. We want you to live your natural span, which is also the right of every doumana, barring accident or illness."

I brushed my hand over Jonton's knee. The touch made me cringe, but I knew it would make her feel connected to me, and more willing to give what I wanted.

"The other thing is the weather machine. It intrigues me. I want to learn everything there is to know about it. How to run it, of course, and how it works, and its history—how it came to be here. Every day I will give my time and myself to you and Pradat, and you will train me on the machine." I handed up a smile. "Seems a fair trade to me, though you gain most of the advantages."

Jonton crossed her arms over her chest.

"It can't be just you with the knowledge," I said, pushing gently. "What if you fall ill, or are injured?"

She waved off the worry with a flick of her hand.

"What you want," I said, pressing on, "is an apprentice. And people to spread the word. It doesn't matter if you can control the weather if no one knows."

Jonton sniffed, and I thought I'd caught her attention, but she turned away and stared into the distance.

"More than that," I said, "you could demonstrate the machine, on the visionstage, to the settled world, with your apprentices beside you. Kler and commune

176

doumanas would see your power and ability, your willingness to teach. They would see that it's you and the orindles who should lead us."

Slowly, so slowly that she could have been mechanical instead of living, Jonton turned her gaze back to me.

"Do you believe the orindles should lead, Khe?"

"A great leader," I said, "shows her power by what she is willing to share."

Jonton laughed quietly. "If I teach you to work the machine, you will endorse our leadership. Who are you that anyone should take your opinion to heart?"

"No one," I said, "but sister to Azlii. You know how corentans are—stubborn for the sake of it. She'll keep quiet just to spite you, but she'll tell the other corentans if I ask her. I am also sister to Larta in Chimbalay, and sister to all those at Lunge commune, which has some influence in the region."

A small smile turned her lips. "You are very clever, Khe. And you make some good points. We'll discuss this more tomorrow."

-=o=-

Pradat walked back to Justice House with me. "Show me your wrist," she said.

I pulled my cloak tighter around me. "It's still drizzling."

She took hold of my elbow through the fabric and stopped, forcing me to stop with her. "Show me your wrist."

I pulled free of her grip. "I checked this morning. All my age spots are still there, all as dark as ever."

"Jonton will want me to accelerate the treatments," Pradat said. "She's not the patient sort."

"Then that's two of us," I said, walking again. "Commemoration is in five days. Very little time left for anyone to be patient."

Pradat tsked her tongue against the roof of her mouth. "I knew you'd feel that way. Knew you'd clap your palm against your thigh when Jonton presented her plan to you. But you have to know that rushing the treatments could have unintended consequences. We could save your life, but leave you a babbler. Or leave your body so weakened that you'd spend your last years moving between your cot and a floating chair."

I stopped again and turned to her. I pitched my voice so only Pradat could hear. I needed to tell someone. "I used to dream all the time. After what the lumani did to me, I didn't dream at all until recently. Now, in my brief sleeps, I have the same dream, night after night. I dream the planet shivers and shakes more mightily than anything we've yet felt. I dream the shiver opens a great mouth in the world, and the mouth swallows me down and then spits me out. After, I'm not Khe any more. I'm something else. Something horrible."

Pradat reached out to touch my neck, but I put my hand up to stop her. I didn't want comforting now. I wanted anger and determination pounding in me. I wanted surety.

"Jonton will starve us all to get what she wants," I said, "and she will always want more. We have to stop her, whatever it takes." I started walking again. "Maybe then I can take what little sleep I need in peace."

Seventeen

Larta drummed her fingers against her thighs—one hand going fast: onetwothreefour, the other moving in counterpoint. One … one … one. My back was to her in the room set up for my treatments. I couldn't see what she was doing, but heard it, the soft pad of skin on the fabric of her hipwrap.

Pradat shifted one of her machines so its light hit the spot where my spine and skull met. The heat, and the drugs dripping into my arms, made my stomach hurt. I closed my eyes and visualized the sky at firstlight, how the colors rose up in the dark to announce the new day. Pain and the nagging pinprick feeling over my body that the treatments brought—worth it all if it bought me more new days. Bought me time to start to rebuild what I'd destroyed.

Jonton was in the room, too. I heard her shuffle a few steps to look at the readouts from Pradat's machines. Jonton didn't like what she saw. I heard it in the way she spit out her breath. I opened my eyes and looked from Pradat to Jonton and back again, but they were too well trained and their necks showed me nothing. The treatment went on.

Once Pradat had unhooked me from her devices, Jonton motioned with her head for us to come with her. I followed her out of the room, down a long hall, to a doorway. Larta came third, favoring her damaged leg. I couldn't see her, but I heard her—the uneven breath of someone unhappy with the situation. She followed behind me so Jonton couldn't see her throat. Not that Larta had feelings in need of hiding—Jonton knew Larta didn't trust her. Why else would she have insisted on sitting in on the treatment?

This was another thing that had come with the destruction of the lumani—sisters questioned each other's motives and actions now. It had been simpler, easier, when we'd all performed our duties without question. When our leaders and *The Rules of a Good Life* made it easy to know and do what was expected. Even when Simanca used *The Rules* to her own advantage, there was at least security. Now there were no rules, and nothing to guide us in this new land.

Jonton opened the door and started down the stairs behind it. I knew where we were now, though we'd come a different route to this place last time. I knew, too, that something of what I'd said to Jonton last night had struck a note in her.

The door to the weather machine room irised open with the barest sound. Larta and I followed her inside.

The machine looked as I remembered it—a huge cube, the color of shadows in the white-on-white room. Its silver dials and levers were placed at just the right height for the average doumana. The long clearstone tube that measured how much rain had fallen was filled to the one-third mark. One-third of what, I wondered? What would full mean?

I hadn't noticed last time, but the machine gave off a faint hum, low-pitched, wavering up and down a few tones, almost like a greeting. Why not a greeting? Wood and stones had consciousness—why not metal? The machine could be happy to have company.

I walked to it and set the palm of one hand against its cool, metallic side. An electric buzz shot across my skin. I jerked my hand back and stared at my palm, expecting to see a burn. Nothing. I touched my palm with the fingers of my other hand. It wasn't even warm.

Jonton's eyebrow ridges drew together. "What happened?"

"I don't know."

She touched the same spot I had, fingertips first, and then with her whole flat hand. Jonton looked at me, and I stared back, my face blank.

The orindle brushed her hand against her green hipwrap, seemingly brushing off her concern for me as well. "Shall we begin your first lesson?"

"I'd like the history first," I said, "how the machine came to be here. You said before that the lumani asked for it to be built after the… problem with the weather-prophets. But I don't understand why."

"Can you not guess?" Jonton said. "Think about it."

I had guesses, but shook my head. I wanted to hear Jonton's version.

"To make our world perfect. Think back, Khe. When is the last time you remember too much or too little rain to grow the crops at Lunge commune? The last time hail destroyed tender stalks? The last time planting was delayed because the sun came late and the soil wasn't warm enough?"

In my lifetime we'd taken for granted planting on a certain date, harvesting a given number of days later.

There were stories, though, at Lunge, about bad years, crop fail years. That was back when every commune had their own weather-prophet, before the lumani centralized the prophets in Chimbalay—before my lifetime, before Simanca's.

Jonton had shifted her gaze to Larta, enjoying her audience, I thought. "When was the last time Chimbalay's streets were drowned in water? Before now, I mean? When was Growing Season ever too hot, or Harvest Season ever anything but pleasantly cool?"

"Never that I remember," Larta said. "But it gets plenty cold every Barren Season."

"For a reason," Jonton said. "There are certain valuable crops that need extreme cold for their roots to form. There are beneficial organisms that only reproduce when the temperature drops below a threshold. The crystals that convert the planet's magnetic field into the electrical power we use to heat and cool, and cook, and run our vehicles only grow if a certain low temperature lasts long enough."

"All from this machine?" I asked.

Jonton stroked the machine's side. "With the weather-prophets we had warning. The lumani could adjust what crops needed to be grown—could hope the necessary organisms would thrive, that the crystals would set properly. With the machine we could guarantee that all conditions would be perfect."

We, she'd said. Not the lumani. Did she consider herself one with them?

"How does the machine work?" I asked.

Jonton drew herself up very straight. "How it works isn't important, only that it does and we can make it do what we want."

I saw that it bothered her, not knowing—because she was an orindle and her life was devoted to the how and why of things. I understood the frustration, and almost felt sorry for her. Almost.

I waved my hand toward the third full water tube. "What do you do with the water? Does it go to the cisterns?"

"Not the cisterns." Jonton seemed relaxed now that she had been asked a question she could answer. "When we set new parameters, the stored water is pumped into the ground to start everything working."

Something I'd noticed before came back to me— that every time the world shook, it was preceded or followed by heavy rain. Maybe pumping water below ground caused the shivers. Because the planet didn't like it? I remembered the sounds I'd heard, like distant sobs, just before a shaking. The sobs—not knowing where they came from, not knowing how to help—felt like a wound to my heart.

"How do you make the machine give you the weather you want?"

"You want me to show you," she said, a statement, not a question.

I shrugged. "I'm curious. And I think it's to your advantage for me to know."

"I disagree," she said. "You need only know what I can do, not how I do it."

"Teach me," I said, taking a step toward her, "because I'm like you—I crave knowledge. Teach me because if you're right and I am becoming something new, then knowing how to work the machine might give me a way to make it work even better. What a gift that would be for you to give your sisters throughout the world—an even better way to control the weather."

I didn't know which of my words moved her, if any. I could have fallen in line with plans she'd already made.

Moments passed, little chips of time that were gone forever.

"Is your memory good, Khe? Controlling the machine isn't simple. You'll have to pay close attention and no doubt we will have to go over this many times." She drew in a breath and huffed it out. "This will be an interesting test. If I am right and your intellect was improved by the powers, you will learn quickly. This will be our first experiment together."

Larta started toward us, likely wanting to see what Jonton was about to show me. Jonton jerked her head to look over her shoulder at Larta. The orindle had let her guard down in those moments that her emotion spots lit, but her training was back in command now.

Her voice was bland as she said, "Larta, would you mind fetching my lead helphand? Her name is Zavren. I'm not sure where she is. You'll have to search for her."

Larta ran her hand over her scalp. It was as obvious to her as to me that Jonton wanted Larta gone while she showed me how to work the machine. It was just as obvious Larta didn't want to leave, but what choice did she have? To refuse without a good reason was unthinkable. It went against every rule of courtesy we'd been raised with—kler or commune. Larta hesitated, then turned and left the room. I heard her footsteps slap against the stairs as she climbed.

Jonton smiled. "Now listen closely, watch what I do, and learn."

-=o=-

It was hard for Larta to hear me in the strong rain, with our hoods pulled up, as we plowed along the nearly deserted streets of Chimbalay. We could have gone back to Justice House, but Larta didn't trust that we'd have privacy there. Not that her guardians would talk, but Jonton seemed to know everything that was said in any structure in Chimbalay, though no one knew how.

"Did you learn how to work the machine?" she asked.

"It's not as hard as Jonton pretends, but it does take precision. But we can't destroy the machine."

"Nothing is perfect," Larta said. "There's a way. We just have to find it."

I wished it were that easy.

"We can't destroy it because we need it. Without it, we'd go back to uncertainty. Hunger in years without enough or too much water. No crystals for heat and power if the Barren Season is too mild."

Larta huffed. "We managed to survive all those generations before the machine. We can do it again."

I turned my face into the rain and let the drops sluice down my skin. "We could, but I can't do it. I destroyed the lumani and threw Chimbalay and our world into disorder. Now Jonton and the orindles want to rule over us. I can't bear to be the cause of more suffering, to do to all doumanas what I've done to

Chimbalay."

"You didn't destroy the lumani alone, Khe."

That was true. But I seemed to be the only one who felt responsible for what Larta, Azlii, Pradat, and I had done, and its aftermath.

We walked without talking, the rain splattering against the stone streets. The first group of doumanas we'd seen since leaving the research center hurried along on the other side of the road, their heads down, hoods pulled up.

"Do you have another idea?" Larta asked. "Or are we to let the orindles take over?"

"I have an idea, but it'll take you and Azlii to make it work. We need the council—more than ever now. Do the orindles still control Presentation House?"

Larta's lips drew into a line before she spoke. "They're still there. My Second has a close sister at Presentation House. She told me today that the orindles now let the technicians run whatever old programs they want, but stop them from sending out anything new unless Jonton orders it."

She seemed to think something over. "My Second says that since the day we found Jonton at Presentation House the technicians rarely leave, and no one is allowed in unless they have approved business there. Approved by the orindles. The only way would be if we rushed in there as a force and took over."

The falling water stopped suddenly, as though a timer had clicked off. I wondered if Jonton had that much control over the weather that she could make rain start and stop exactly at her whim. I pushed the hood of my cloak back. Rushing Presentation House

186

might work, but I had a different target for the guardians in mind.

We walked in silence a few minutes, coming to a break in the street, a choice to keep on the way we'd been going, take a different route, or turn back and return to the research center. I dropped back a pace, to let Larta take the lead, but she stopped and turned to me.

"Jonton isn't going to quietly step aside."

"No, she won't. By the time the representatives get here, we'll need to have Jonton contained."

She hiked up her eyebrow ridges. "Contained?"

"I've thought about this. Jonton's become a babbler. No sane doumana would risk starving her sisters to gain power. Kelroosh found hatchlings left at a mating site. Just left there. Either the doumanas who should have gone for them forgot, or someone told them not to bother. Either way, things are terribly wrong in Chimbalay."

Doumanas were returning to the streets in large numbers now that the rain had stopped. I pulled up my hood again and drew it tight around my face. I leaned close to Larta and lowered my voice. "Jonton and the orindles and helphands who have sided with her need to be dealt with as you would any babbler in Chimbalay."

Larta stared at me. "These are our sisters. One babbler, yes, for the good and harmony of the community, would be turned out to the wilderness. But you can't send them all. We need orindles and helphands."

"Then what instead?"

A group of doumanas was coming our way. I ducked my head as they approached.

When they had passed, Larta said, "The guardians will come for Jonton. We'll remove anyone who springs to her defense and hold her at Justice House. I won't do more than that against my own kler-sister."

Eighteen

Larta fiddled with the bracelets on her wrists, the ones with the symbols of her work and rank embossed on them. "I don't like this. We guardians exist more to help than anything else. We only have stunners in case beasts from the wilderness threaten our sisters while they go to and from visiting corentas. I've never used one to threaten a doumana."

"Not even a babbler?"

Larta shook her head. "The babblers all went quietly. Even Marnka, for all the trouble she'd caused. In the end she went out the gates without a fuss."

When I'd stayed with Marnka in the wilderness she'd told me she'd pushed an orindle out a second floor window, breaking her leg. Marnka was proud of what she'd done and felt no sorrow for having harmed a sister. The same way that Jonton felt no sorrow at the harm she did her sisters in Chimbalay and to soumyo all over the planet. Maybe it was loss of compassion that made doumanas insane. Maybe that was the definition of insanity—the inability to care about others.

"I hope we won't need a stunner with Jonton, but best to be prepared."

Larta sighed again, and picked up a weapon from those lying on a table. She slipped it into a leather pocket shaped like the instrument in the special cloak she'd put on. She nodded to the nine other guardians. The brownish-pink of uncertainty showed on a few necks, but softly. Each guardian chose a stunner and slipped it into the pocket of her cloak. Duty was the stronger emotion, bred into us over the generations that the lumani had ruled our world.

I felt my neck warm. Here was another consequence of having destroyed the lumani: sister turning against sister. It had to be put right.

-=o=-

I'd worried that Jonton would use the machine against us, opening the skies and pouring driving rain on our heads. I didn't doubt she knew we were coming. However her information network operated, it was efficient. The late afternoon sky stayed clear, but when I looked up the sun was shady and weak, as pale as old yolks.

Could Jonton control that too? Not the sun, but the air somehow, how we perceived the world around us? I shivered in the warming air.

"What?" Larta asked, as we walked side by side.

"Nothing," I said. "A thought. Nothing real to worry about."

One of the guardians stepped up on Larta's other side. "Some of our sisters are nervous about bringing the stunners. They're wondering what we'll be up against."

Larta kept her steps as steady as her damaged leg allowed, but I saw swirling within her the brownish-pink of uncertainty and the dark-gray-purple of the frustration uncertainty brought.

"I don't know any more than what I told them at Justice House," she said. "Jonton and any orindles— or anyone else—who tries to stop us from taking control of the machine will be detained and removed. That's our job, and we'll do it. We're not—"

The sudden sob seemed to come from beneath our feet. A sob like I'd heard back in Research Center Three, though no one else seemed to hear it then. I stopped and listened.

"What—" Larta said, but was cut off by a loud rumble through the air.

The ground beneath us buckled and rolled. Yips of surprise came from the guardians behind us. Larta grabbed my arm and the shoulder of the guardian on her other side, trying to keep herself from falling. I set my feet wide and bent my knees to keep balanced. I held onto Larta to keep her and the other guardian from tumbling down, amazed that I was strong enough to do it.

The shiver passed in a moment. The sky was still bright, but rain fell as hard and sudden as an avalanche. The guardians who had been behind us squeezed up and we grouped together, each of us tugging our hoods over our heads. I glanced around the street and saw groups of other doumanas doing the same, most walking fast now, in a hurry to reach their destinations.

Larta stepped in front of our group and held up a hand dripping with rain. "Jonton seems to be sending us a greeting. Or perhaps she felt the gardens were dry and in need of a soak. Either way, we do what we have come to do. We do it like guardians—peaceably, orderly, with the best wishes for our sisters in our hearts, but prepared."

She reached into her pocket. I saw her fingers moving inside. The other guardians reached into their pockets and their fingers moved in the same practiced motions.

-=o=-

Many of the public structures in Chimbalay had stone steps leading to wide porches, but Research Center Three had more steps than most, more than twice as many. We climbed the twenty-three steps and I realized the reason this first floor was so high was to make space for the machine below, which didn't make sense if this structure had been built for the lumani when they had Chimbalay constructed, long before the mistakes of the weather-prophets and the building of the machine. Had Jonton lied about when and why the machine was built, or had the lumani put the machine here because there was existing room? What else might be hidden in this place? I wished the structures of Chimbalay would communicate. Things would be much easier if I could ask and they would answer.

The rain beat down, as hard as pebbles. No orindles or helphands were out on the porch. Larta didn't knock or call out; she aimed her stunner at a small depression beside the door, fired a light-bolt, and the door irised open. She held up, rather than bursting in, stepping carefully into the barely lit foyer.

"Empty." She motioned us in with a wave of her hand.

The door to the large receiving room flew open. An

192

orindle I didn't recognize stood between the jambs, her fists on her hips, her elbows jutting to the sides. The brown-yellow of annoyance showed on her throat. I wondered why she'd chosen to show us her feelings.

"Kith," Larta said, naming the orindle, "step aside and let us in."

Larta's neck showed nothing. This was her work and she did it well. It didn't cause strong emotion in her. Or wouldn't, if Kith stepped aside quickly. If not...

It didn't take lumani hearing to know there were more doumanas inside the room. They scraped chairs and moved around, and some gave little gasps. I worried about how many might be behind the door, if they would try to stop us.

"Kith," Larta said, using the doumana's name again to bring the orindle's focus to her, "*The Rules of a Good Life* say, 'Trust in those who keep you safe and obey their every request.' You know what has to happen. You and the others must go with the guardians back to Justice House."

Kith stood a moment longer, colors blooming and fading out on her throat as she thought through her options. Finally the pale-yellow-blue of acceptance replaced the other colors and she sighed, pleased, I thought, not to have to make a stand. It was the way we were—trained to *The Rules* and content to follow them. I thought again of what Thedra had said—that we were like flocking birds. Give us a leader—any leader, even a guardian—and we would happily follow.

Larta cocked her head slightly to the left, waiting. Kith stepped out of the doorway.

I quickly counted seven orindles in their green hipwraps, and four helphands in yellow. None of them looked inclined to quarrel. Several bore the soft-green-yellow of relief on their throats.

Larta glanced toward a knot of guardians. "Take them to Justice House, where they'll be safe."

The orindles and helphands started moving through the door. The room had emptied, leaving only Larta, five remaining guardians, Kith, and me. Kith moved slowly toward the door, perhaps regretting now her acceptance of Larta's orders.

Larta grabbed her elbow. "Where is Jonton?"

Kith gave her a sour look and kept silent.

"Larta," I said, "it's raining."

The guardian glanced at me, her look now as sour as Kith's.

"It's raining hard," I said. "There's only one place Jonton could be—with the machine."

-=o=-

Larta forced open the door to the machine room with a shot from her stunner, holding her free arm back, her palm facing down, to tell us to halt. The only other time I'd seen Larta at her work was when she'd found me scavenging something to eat from one of Chimbalay's refuse area. She'd been kind then, and still she'd scared me. Now she was tight, her muscles taut. She took a quick look around, straightened, and walked into the room. Her hand moved to her pocket.

"Jonton," she said as the rest of us followed her in.

The orindle turned away from the machine and bared her teeth at us. Her neck was awash with the brown-black of anger, but also the red-purple of amusement. How could she be amused? She was a babbler, her rational mind gone. I'd seen what power could do—saw it turn Simanca cold-necked and unfaithful to her sisters. Power had driven Jonton insane.

Had I unleashed this, too, on my community? Jonton's ambition. I didn't want to believe it. Didn't believe it. The destruction of the lumani had given us freedom. What we did with that freedom was up to each of us.

Jonton's back was to a wall. Several gray cylinders the width of my two hands around jutted from the barrier. The cylinders hadn't been there before, or had been, but were hidden. I couldn't guess what they were for. The guardians stood in a semicircle around her, their hands in their pockets, ready to reach for their weapons.

Larta stepped forward. "Jonton, we've come to protect you."

The orindle turned and reached inside the cylinder closest to her. Every guardian tensed. Their fingers twitched in their pockets.

Jonton pulled a slim black hose from within the cylinder and pointed it to the left side of Larta. She pressed on the hose, a certain spot, a button perhaps. A shimmering jet of sharp blue light shot across the room. The guardian to Larta's left cried out, threw her arms across her chest, and fell to the floor.

Larta dropped to her knees by her sister, her fingers on the doumana's throat, touching each emotion spot one by one. The room was unnaturally quiet, as though the air and all the life had been sucked from it. Larta looked up, her eyes stricken. But I'd already known the fallen doumana no longer lived. We all knew.

No one moved—every doumana as still as stone. Every neck burning with the gray-red of shock. We had no word for what Jonton had done, the deliberate Returning of a doumana—no word for a thing that went against every *Rule* and rightness of our lives. Even Jonton seemed stunned, her throat the same mass of gray-red as the guardians' necks. Maybe she hadn't known what the hose would do. Maybe she'd thought it would merely knock someone back, or daze them at the worst.

Then movement—to my right. A guardian yanked her weapon from her cloak and leveled it at Jonton. The guardian's face was hard, her eyes wide, the spots on her neck the red-pink of certainty.

Jonton must have caught the movement too, caught the colors on the doumana's neck as well. She fired the hose again. The doumana screamed and fell, her stunner clattering on the floor.

The machine suddenly hummed loudly and banged. Two guardians jumped toward Jonton. Jonton squeezed the hose and both doumanas fell.

Everything had happened so quickly I could hardly take it in.

"Enough," Jonton yelled, and I didn't know if she meant that anyone who attacked her would also fall, or that she didn't want to hurt anyone else. I wanted it to be the second, wanted Jonton not to have gone completely insane, not to be a babbler who would destroy her sisters without thought or remorse.

196

"What now?" Larta stepped forward, but kept her hand in her pocket. Her voice was calm, but her neck showed anger, and nerves, and the bright-greenish-blue of a wanting hope.

Hope, I thought, because Larta, too, wanted there to be no more doumanas Returned or damaged. Wanted to stop Jonton without hurting her. To end the rain.

Jonton glared. Her breath came fast, and she pointed the hose toward Larta. Larta froze where she stood.

"The lumani planned for this," Jonton said. "They knew a day might come when the comforts and order they provided would be thrown away by foolish doumanas. They had protections built. I learned to use them, just as I learned to work the weather machine." She glanced down at the hose, then back at Larta. "You will leave now. All of you except Khe."

Larta hissed a stream of air between her teeth, but she turned and nodded, and watched her one remaining guardian walk up the steps and out, until only she was left. Larta threw a last glance at Jonton and started walking slowly toward the door, nearly bumping into me. Her hand grazed mine, slipping the stunner into my palm. Heart pounding, I closed my fingers tight around the instrument.

The low hum from the weather machine suddenly rose in pitch and loudness. Jonton glanced toward it, and I swung my arm up, leveling the stunner at her chest. Her eyes flicked back to me and grew wide. In that small beat of time Larta turned, ran back, and flung herself at the orindle, knocking her to the ground. They

197

landed with a hard thud, Larta on top.

"Stay down, Jonton," I said, pointing the stunner at her. I had no idea how to work it, but she didn't know that. I *hoped* she didn't know that.

Larta rolled away and pulled herself up into a sit. Her teeth were clenched so tightly I thought they might break from the pressure. She held her hand out to me. I gave her the stunner, glad to be rid of it, but afraid of what she might do. She glared at Jonton.

"There's still this," I said, to distract them both, and slid my gaze toward the weather machine, and then to the water-level gauge, which was nearly filled to the top. It must have been storming hard the whole time we were in this room.

"I don't trust her to touch it," Larta said as she got to her feet. She kept the stunner pointed at Jonton.

The orindle turned her head to look up at Larta, and smiled.

"I can do it, I think," I said quickly, before Larta's anger could rise up again. "She showed me enough. I can at least stop the rain for now."

"I won't hurt her," Larta said. "Not unless she gives me cause." She took a deep breath. "Let's see what you can do, Khe. Let's stop the rain."

The machine stood stark in the tired air. The silver dials, Jonton had said, were only there for show. The secret of the machine was in changing whispers of air. Very exact whispers, more like the sound of breath than words, and precise hand movements. Something the lumani wouldn't have been able to do, without the help of a doumana. I didn't understand how it worked, but the how didn't matter, only precision.

I swallowed and hoped I remembered the exact sequence Jonton had showed me, the exact pronunciation of the sounds. I stepped up to the machine and spoke, softly, the way I might to a frightened hatchling, being careful to remember the sounds in order, to remember the hand motions in order. I couldn't guess at what the wrong word or motion might make the machine do. Maybe nothing. Maybe something that could never be put right again.

I saw Larta from the corner of my eye, her posture straight and tense. Jonton sat on the floor, as loose as a dangling thread, her arms around her drawn up knees, watching me. There seemed to be a look of expectation in her eyes. I leaned close to the machine and said the words, while my hands moved in the dance Jonton had showed me. When I was done, I stepped back.

I expected the machine to lurch, make a sound, click off, something. The only sound was the rush of water into the gauge, a gauge that would soon overflow, flooding the room.

"I was right," Jonton said. "Everything about you is changing. It took me almost from moon to moon to learn the words and the sequence that you saw once and repeated perfectly."

I turned and glared at her. If I'd done it so well, why was the rain still falling just as hard? Had she tricked me? Seen ahead to this moment and taught me the wrong thing?

Except that the sound in the water gauge was changing. It was slight. So slight I was sure Larta and Jonton couldn't have caught it. But I did. The drops hitting with less force. The water slowing its swirl.

"You'd better hope she was perfect." Larta's voice was cold, each word precise. "We'll be standing here waiting until the rain completely stops. And then it's off to Justice House, where your sisters are waiting. And justice there will be, for my fallen sisters."

Jonton pursed her lips, but nodded. The fight seemed to have gone out of her. Gone, or maybe curled away, waiting for the best moment to strike.

Marnka had been this way in the wilderness—a mad babbler one moment, calm the next.

"We can go now," I said, my head tilted, my ear hole cocked toward the gauge. "The rain is slowing. It will stop."

"You're sure?" Larta asked, her eyes never leaving Jonton.

I lifted my shoulders in a shrug. "I'm sure." And was sure, though I couldn't have said why.

Larta accepted that, and motioned to Jonton. "Get up. We're going now."

Jonton didn't ease herself up, she leapt. And jumped sideways, then crouched, her hands on the ground on either side of her feet, as if she might pounce.

Larta fired her stunner. The burst missed Jonton and hit the machine. Sparks flew. Smoke tumbled from the machine, filling the room. I bent over, coughing. I could hear Larta and Jonton coughing as well, and then the sound of only two coughing—Larta and me. The smoke began to clear. Larta stood alone, her face redder than usual, panting. She swung her gaze, scanning the room.

"Where'd she go?"

I shook my head. "Where *could* she go? I didn't hear her moving. Or the door open."

The guardian's eyes flickered around the room, lingered on her fallen sisters. I saw how her breath caught in her chest, how she made herself breathe again.

"A trick door," Larta said, slipping the stunner back into its pocket. "I can't think of any other answer."

I was sure now the lumani hadn't built this room. What use would they—who could be visible or invisible to doumanas as they chose—have of a hidden escape route? If doumanas had made the trick door, then we could find it.

"Tell me what she did," I said.

Larta made little tsking sounds as she thought. "I couldn't see much in the smoke." She ran her hand over her scalp. "I remember now. I know what she did—she bent down like this."

Larta scooted over a couple of hand's-breadths and squatted, imitating Jonton's stance, and tapped her fingers on the floor, moving slowly up and down by her feet.

"I don't know exactly where she touched," Larta said. "There's nothing on the ground that I can see that looks like an opening."

I hunkered down a little ways from her and let my vision go loose, trying to see with lumani eyes. The floor was crisscrossed with scrapes of different colors. I wasn't sure what the colors meant, but I was glad to see them. They didn't match up with emotions that I could tell. There were pink trails, the color of nurturing, and that made no sense. Pale-yellow-blue formed a puddle in one spot, but I didn't think acceptance was an emotion either doumana had felt during their struggle.

"You're sure this is the spot she disappeared from?"

"I'm sure," Larta said, still tapping her fingers along the floor. "More or less."

"Stop," I said, remembering something I'd heard while the smoke had clogged my eyes. "Not like that. Like this." I moved next to Larta and tapped my fingers on the floor in the rhythm I'd heard.

In a blink, Larta was gone.

There'd been no sound. I hadn't seen her go.

I stared at the empty spot on the floor where she'd been. Sweat prickled my body, crown to sole. I couldn't let her go to wherever she'd gone alone.

My hand was still on the spot I'd last touched. I pressed my fingers into the floor and carefully sidled around to squat where Larta had been. I tapped the rhythm.

NINETEEN

The small room where I found myself was formed from compacted reddish dirt, flat on the bottom, with rounded sides and ceiling. It must have been dug out from the space below the machine room, which was below the research center. Probably we'd all landed in the same spot—first Jonton, then Larta, then me—slipping into a musty, underground world. I'd had no sense of motion. Just one place one moment, another place the next. I didn't know how that was possible.

The slap, slap of running feet moving away from where I'd landed jolted me back to *why* I was here. I hauled myself to my feet and hurried after the sound—out of the small room, into a passageway.

The passage wasn't wide. I probably could have touched both sides by extending my arms. Standing on my toes, my arms straight above my head, I might have reached the ceiling. The cavern was dry though. However deep below ground we were, water didn't seep in. A vein of clearstone ran through the red dirt, about my shoulder height, reflecting the glow from the tiny luminescent creatures that wriggled through the soil. The glow lit the passage in a soft-white light. Two sets of faint footprints marred the dirt.

The passage bent. I couldn't see who was running—only heard the steps moving away—but guessed it had to be Larta chasing Jonton. The sound of running feet faded. I tried to gauge how far ahead Larta would have to be for me not to hear her any more. I could hear a long distance, but things twisted and turned here, the passage seeming to spiral in on itself, then jut out in a new direction. There were plenty of other passages breaking off from the one I was following. Jonton and Larta could have gone down one of them. Or several of them, if more passages broke off from the first one.

I tried to see their trail with lumani vision. I had begun to think I'd got some control over the vision, could make it work when I wanted. I saw nothing but dirt.

I stopped a moment and listened hard. Was that something, there, to the left? A shout? I held my breath and opened my mouth slightly, to hear better.

Nothing.

I rubbed my hand over my face, thinking. I could wait here. Whoever was running would have to come back this way. Except there could be other exits. In truth, I didn't know where any exits were—or if there were an exit. The trip underground might be one way.

The footprints in the dirt had disappeared. The soil was too hard here for the faint impressions to show. Or maybe Larta had chased Jonton down a side route. I turned and crept back the way I'd come, bent over at the waist, looking for another set of prints to join the ones I'd left.

I found them at an opening jutting off to the right. Two sets—one flat-footed, the other toes only, a runner. I wanted to run too. My energy level was ramping up now, here, below ground. I thought maybe it was the planet's doing, the way—since the lumani had changed me—that the planet nourished me, so I rarely ate, drank, or slept. That deep into the world as I was now, the planet gave me more than I gained through bare feet on raw soil.

Another shout echoed against the walls. I was sure this time it was a shout. It came from somewhere ahead. Now I had sounds to follow I ran. Mad sounds—grunting and shrieks, the ugly noise of flesh striking flesh. My neck grew hot from fear and worry. I came around a corner and saw them.

Larta and Jonton rolled together on the ground, each desperate for the top position, both of their necks aglow with the black-blue of determination. I froze where I stood. Doumanas didn't do this. Young beastlets, I'd seen them rolling and tumbling with each other, fighting, but not doumanas. It wasn't in our nature. Hadn't been in our nature.

Larta seemed to have won for the moment—she had her hands crossed on Jonton's chest, holding her down. She leaned low, as if to say something in the orindle's ear hole.

Jonton bit hard into Larta's shoulder, and Larta yelled. Crimson drops rose on her skin in the shape of the orindle's teeth. In the eye blink when Larta lost concentration from the pain and surprise, Jonton shoved her hard, throwing Larta onto her back, and climbed on her chest. The orindle drew her arm back. Her hand squeezed tight and Jonton slammed her fist hard into Larta's jaw. The guardian's head lay at an awkward angle on her neck.

A hot flame streaked down my chest at that sound,

at what I'd seen. Anger roiled through me, as fierce as any I'd ever felt. Jonton jumped up and, before I could grab her, she ran down the passageway—not the way we'd come, but deeper into what was unknown.

I didn't think. I chased after Jonton, determined to bring her down and back to Larta. Jonton's lead was slight. Her neck was still lit black-blue, but the blue-red of anxiety had bloomed there as well. She should have been anxious. However single-minded she was to escape, I was more resolute that she wouldn't. I ran hard until I was within an arm's length of her. I leapt toward her back, wrapped my arms around her and hauled her to the ground. The whoosh of air streaming out of her lungs as she landed was strangely satisfying. I didn't like that it made me happy.

I thought I heard Larta puffing, running up. Jonton and I rolled on the ground, shifting direction, and tumbled into a new room—dirt floor, but stone walls, not like the other rooms. I held Jonton down, pinning her shoulders to the dirt

I felt a soft knee in my back, Larta nudging me aside. I wished again that my spots would light—to show Larta how happy I was to see she was fine. She grabbed Jonton by the arm and pulled her to her feet. In Larta's free hand was the stunner, pointed at Jonton.

I turned, and gasped at the room.

It was the size of the huge receiving room in Research Center Three. I thought maybe we were directly under that room, this one a mirror space—but that room, the one above, held furniture and open space.

This room held floating faces.

"What is this place?" Larta asked. Her voice quivered in a way I'd never heard from her before. Bold Larta, as shaken as I was.

The faces floated in three distinct areas, as if they didn't belong together, but they were all doumanas and males. The faces were slightly transparent, not like on a visionstage where you'd swear you could touch the doumana speaking, and it was only faces, not whole bodies—face after face, suspended in the air like hanging balls. They made my stomach queasy, and yet I couldn't help searching for a face that was familiar. None were.

I sensed Larta come up next to me, warmth radiating from her skin from the run. The blood, where Jonton had bitten her, had stopped flowing and was starting to dry. She held Jonton tight by the arm, though the orindle seemed in no mood to run.

"I know her," Larta said.

"Who?"

She jutted her chin toward one of the floating faces. "She lives in Chimbalay. I don't know her well. I think her name is Gunt. She's a technician at Presentation House." Larta took another step forward, pulling Jonton with her. "I know him, too. He was a male I didn't choose at my first Resonance. He tried hard, though."

I stared at the faces, an idea crystallizing in my mind. I wanted to touch them, but was afraid to, as if they might pop like bubbles in boiling water. "I think I know what this is. We keep accounts like this of the plants and preslets at Lunge. It's a breeding record."

"Very good, Khe," Jonton said.

Irritation churned in me at her tone, but I kept silent. Larta's annoyance was more obvious, glowing brown-black on her neck. It was only her training as a guardian, I supposed, that kept Larta from doing something she'd regret.

"I know how it works," Jonton said. "Would you like to see who came before you? Who you made?"

"I'd like to see you get us out of here," Larta said, her patience clearly running as thin as water now.

I'd never thought about how I came to be. Two unknown soumyo had mated; I had come from the egg they'd made. I had wondered if my offspring might have inherited some of my grower's talent, but there was no way to know, so I'd not dwelled on the question. Now, I did want to know. Desperately.

"Can you show me?" I asked Jonton.

She smiled and took a tentative step away from Larta, who reluctantly let her.

"Like this," Jonton said, moving her hands in a complicated rhythm over a green panel. "We'll find you, shall we? Khe of Lunge commune."

Something in the room clicked and whirred. My face came up, small as a seed at first, then growing to life-sized. It chilled me to see it. To one side were two other faces, one doumana, one male. Nice enough looking, both with skin the same shade as mine, but strangers. They meant nothing to me. On the other side, another face came up. Male. His eyes were the same shape and color as mine. I didn't know what the two sides meant. Once we emerge, we look the same through our lifetimes. The male and female on one side could be my progenitors or my offspring. The male on the other side could be either as well. I gazed at the faces—no different than seeing a stranger's face on the streets of Chimbalay. A fourth face came up.

"Trah!" Larta's voice rang with surprise.

My heart banged in my chest. I stepped toward the face I knew so well.

Nez.

"If this is a breeding record," Larta said, "then Nez is your offspring."

Heat flashed through me. I knew what Larta said was true. Perhaps I'd already known it. The bond I felt with Nez was different from what I felt with any of my other sisters, stronger. The gold cord I sometimes saw reaching from one of us to the other—I'd never seen that with anyone else.

"The lumani tracked everything," Jonton said. "Generation after generation, every mating. They tracked the eggs. When hatchlings left the egg, the lumani used the records to decide where to place them. They thought that looking at the progenitors could predict what a doumana or male would be good at in their lives."

I knew the lumani saw us as some grand experiment, but this shook me to my core. The lumani had made us, made me, made every single doumana and male then alive what they were. None of what had happened after their destruction was my fault. It simply was what we were—what they had made us. Some were brave, and some fearful, and some wanted nothing more than to be left with their sisters to do their work. And some wanted power so great that it rivaled the lumani themselves.

209

The room felt suddenly close, unstable—as though the ceiling might crash down at any moment.

Nez was my offspring.

"Do you know the way out?" I asked Jonton.

"I know every secret of Research Center Three. Every secret of the Powers."

Larta jerked the orindle's arm—fed up, I thought, as I was, with Jonton's brags. "Come on. Show us."

Jonton stood her ground. "There's something else here Khe might like to know about."

"Just Khe?" Larta said.

"In this case." Jonton stared at me, her eyes focused on mine, the moments passing away, growing as stale as the air in that underground room.

"This is a place of power," she said.

Larta sniffed. "The lumani had Chimbalay built for them. Yes, we know."

Jonton's smile was tight. "Not The Powers, the lumani. *Power.* Power for The Powers, I suppose."

"We should leave now," I said, a fresh nervousness pounding through me.

"Have you never wondered why Chimbalay was built here?" Jonton asked. "It's an odd place for a kler, wilderness all around. The nearest commune or neighboring kler is many days' walk away. No other place is set off the way Chimbalay is, not even the nesting grounds."

Larta still had hold of one of Jonton's arms. Her hand tightened slightly around it.

"Your story better be good," the guardian said. "I'm getting tired of being underground. I want to get out of here."

Jonton's eyes tracked to where Larta's hand was squeezing her arm, then back to me. "Chimbalay was built where it is because the lumani recognized that this is a natural power spot, a place where the magnetic energies of the planet come together and concentrate."

She twisted slightly, pulling away from Larta's hold. Larta let her, but shot Jonton a look that clearly said if the orindle tried to escape she wouldn't get far—and would be the worse for it.

Subtle shifts, I thought—Larta so curious she was willing to give up a slice of control. The need to know thrumming in me like insects trapped in a bottle. Jonton loose, her stance like an instructor on the visionstage, her voice pitched to carry.

"We know our planet has magnetic fields," Jonton said. "We use them to navigate to our nesting sites. But there are also peculiarities, locations where the magnetic forces of the planet intersect and intensify. This is one of them."

She paused, and looked disappointed that neither Larta nor I said anything, or even moved.

"There's a smaller one under Lunge commune, as it happens."

Still neither Larta nor I spoke.

"The Powers, the lumani," Jonton said, "have long life spans, much longer than ours, but not as long naturally as they managed to eke out here. They fed on electricity, but what sustained them, what gave them life, was the planet itself. They built Chimbalay where the force was strongest."

I nodded unconsciously, then noticed I'd done it. I'd already reasoned that, after the lumani had changed

me, it was the planet that became my food and drink—
that kept me alive. I always felt better with my feet on
the ground. When Simanca had thrown me into the
underground root cache and I'd lain in the dark for
what seemed a long time, I was stronger than I had
been in a while. Here, in this place, deep below the
surface, I felt better and healthier than I ever
remembered feeling.

Jonton leaned toward me. "There is a place here,
Khe, that sits at the heart of the junction."

Larta tsked her tongue against the roof of her
mouth. "There'll be no trade here. No special room for
Khe in exchange for letting you go, much less for
letting you have whatever leadership role it is you
crave."

Two spots lit gray-green on Jonton's throat.
"You're taking the wrong trail, guardian. It's not a trade
I'm after. I'm an orindle, not some corentan or
commune leader haggling over the price of preslets or
how many seeds I'll trade for the latest gossip. It's not
a trade I'm after. What I want is for Khe to have her
time back. To live long enough to become what she
will be. To be with her when it happens and after."

I stared at the orindle. What was Jonton really after?

"Seems to me that'd be up to her," Larta said.
"Though I'm sure she'd like to see this place, this
heart."

My throat closed up and I couldn't speak, only nod.
I wanted to see the room if it would truly give me back
my life. But if this room did what Jonton said, why had
she been so insistent that I continue Pradat's
treatments? Why not bring me there to begin with?

I asked the questions.

Jonton sighed. "Pradat's treatments aren't working."

Heat streamed up my breastbone. Then I saw the truth of things.

"You counted on the treatments not working." I said.

"I know many, many secrets of the lumani," Jonton said, "but I don't know where the heart is. But you, Khe, you who are becoming lumani, perhaps you can find it."

My neck burned. Was I *becoming* lumani? Not just something in between, not something neither doumana nor lumani, but turning into the thing I hated? I dragged the back of my hand across my mouth, as though that could wipe away the fear growing in me.

"How?" I said. "What Weast did to me, it didn't give me the lumani's memories, or their knowledge. All it did…" Was what? Maybe gave me some insight. Or maybe that came with the Resonance surgery that unlocked my ability to push the crops. Maybe that unlocking had brought me other things as well.

The ability to see into Jonton's heart.

"You want it for yourself," I said. "You hope it will turn back time. How could anything do that, Jonton? How could it give you years that aren't yours to have? You're not like me. I want back only what was stolen. You want something that was never meant to be yours."

She leaned toward me. "Why should we return during our thirty-fifth year? I've watched my sisters in their last year try not to resent what they couldn't avoid. Watched my sisters, as vibrant and as valuable as ever, Return only because of age. What is lost to us, Khe, when our sisters are gone? What might they have discovered? What good and wonderful things might they have done? It's wrong that we must Return simply because the world has spun a certain number of times. You, Khe, if you find the heart, you could give all your sisters—and brothers—more time to do great things."

I remembered Hwanta, at Lunge commune—so many years past and still her screams were fresh in my ears—crying out the creator was cruel and cheated us, to take our lives while we were still healthy and wanting to give. How could I blame Jonton for her desire? When Weast had offered me nearly twice my normal life span, I'd grabbed at it with greedy hands.

Larta blew out a breath. "More time for the council to lead this world forward."

"More time for we orindles to lead."

The gray-green of revulsion showed on Larta's neck, but her voice was calm. "But you will share this new wonder with all the soumyo?"

Jonton turned to me. "It's a room. The lumani spoke of it. I'm sure it's here, in the caverns, but for all the time I've spent looking, I could never find it. But you can. For you, the room is your best hope."

Best hope. Jonton had no idea what would happen in that room.

My mouth felt dry and my hands shook. I knew *less* than Jonton where this heart might be. She, at least, knew where it wasn't.

A soft rumble caught my ears. I saw that Jonton and

Larta heard it, too. We'd learned what that sound meant and braced ourselves but the mad shaking we'd expected didn't come. The ground rolled once beneath our feet, slow and gentle, like a dream, and stopped.

Larta said something, but her words were hidden by a sound I'd never heard before—like a single raindrop quickly hitting a small hollow log over and over again, so fast that no beast could run as quickly as those drops fell. Larta's mouth was moving, and Jonton's to answer her. I could tell they didn't hear what I heard. A whoosh, like a huge wind, streamed through the cavern, but there was no wind. The sound of rain on wood returned.

An old sound joined—every kind of bird chirping, squawking, calling at the same time in thousands of voices. There were words in the chittering and squawking. Words I understood, but couldn't say how I did—my name being called. Warmth spread through me, from the soles of my feet, climbing upward. Warmth and contentment. And knowledge. The words leading me, saying, *Come*, *Khe. This way. Come to me.*

I stumbled out of the record room, following the voice like chasing a trail of smoke. The rain and wind sounds died away. I heard Larta behind me tsk and Jonton gasp, and two sets of footsteps rushing to catch up.

The tiny creatures that lit the passageway glowed brighter now than before, lighting the red rocks with a white fire flowing through the walls. Larta took my arm. I shook her off, as if her touch would dampen the words I strained now to hear.

This passage, *Khe. Turn east here.*

I turned without looking and knocked over a little tower of rocks, the stones scattering. Larta cried out. Some stones must have landed on her foot. I couldn't stop now, not even for Larta.

The voice pulled me onward.

Downward. Deeper and deeper into the world. The air grew cold—which was odd, since I'd seen on the visionstage how doumanas at the mining communes sweated deep underground. I followed the voice's directions into a long passage so thin the rough walls rubbed against both my shoulders.

There were hardly any of the glowing creatures in the dirt here. I could barely see an arm's length in front of my eyes. Larta and Jonton were still behind me, but I heard their footsteps falter, unsure in the darkness. I hoped they'd stop following. Wherever I was being led, it seemed right that I should come alone.

Almost there, the voice that was like thousands of chittering birds said, *the mouth is soon*.

The passage walls were so tight I had to squeeze my shoulders together and twist to walk sideways. The walls crumbled away where I pushed through, dirt falling down my back and chest. Small rocks tore at my skin. The way was almost perfectly dark. My heart pounded. Commune-raised, my world was always wide open. Sweat beaded above my lips. My neck burned. I pushed on.

The scent of sweet air told me something was changing. A few more steps, and there was nothing on my right shoulder, where the passage wall had been so tight before. I took a few more steps before turning toward the black void—the opening to another passage. *The mouth*, the voice had said. I blinked, nervous, and walked into the emptiness.

As I walked the walls began to glow again from the luminescent creatures, the light growing stronger the further I went. The cavern was large enough that all my commune-sisters could have stood in it comfortably. At the back was a rectangular metal door—the only door I'd seen since we'd left the machine room.

I stood staring at it, hearing hard breathing behind me as Larta and Jonton squeezed their way through the last tight steps, and gasps when the wall fell away on their right. I reached out, but there was no way to open the door that I could see. Larta and Jonton came up beside me.

"You've found it," Jonton said. Her emotion spots glowed crimson in happiness.

Larta's neck showed blue-red with worry.

"I can't figure the door," I said. "All this way, to be stopped by a door…"

Jonton's lips turned in a bare smile and she stepped forward. "The door is to keep the power contained." She waved her hand over a small indentation in the dirt walls. The door clicked and then slid away, sinking sideways into the dirt wall.

It was just a room, dirt walls like all the others, though the soil was dark, dark-red with wide swatches of black running through it. The same kind of tiny, luminous creatures that had lit our way in the rest of the cavern glowed here too. My shoulders drew up and a tremble ran across them. My skin itched, a feeling like I'd drenched myself in mud and it had tightened as it dried. My earholes buzzed and I swiped at them with my hands.

Jonton watched me with a bland curiosity. I knew I was an experiment to her, as I'd been to the lumani. Her only desire was to see what would happen—her small hope that it would be something she could use for herself.

I didn't want to step into that room, not now, not ever.

I wanted to run in, shut the door behind me, throw my head back and my arms out and soak up whatever was in there like bread in water.

I thought of Nez. A strange concept—to *know* my offspring and discover a new kind of love, different and beyond what I felt for my sisters: a bond so deep it had its own color, a bond that made me desperate to see how her life turned out.

I thought of Larta, and Azlii, and Pradat, of how much I wanted to see them and share in their lives, my good sisters, for more than just the time left before Commemoration Day; my best chance, to have what I'd given so much for, lay in the room beyond.

I stepped across the threshold.

Twenty

The door whizzed closed behind me. The room was bare, since the lumani had no need for chairs or pillows. The air smelt different here, musty and stagnant like everywhere else in this cavern, but salty too—so salty I could taste it. The acrid scent of Weast and the other lumani, faint as a whisper, echoed from the air and soil. Of course it would smell like them here. The lumani came here, who knew how often? Often enough to have lived through generation after generation of soumyo.

A shudder ran up my spine—remembering Weast, what he'd done to me. The sense of burning from the inside out as the unnatural egg it had grown in me slid down my channel. The relief when the egg fell onto the floor, a mass of nothing.

I ran my hand over my scalp and flicked my wrist to throw the memory away.

I walked through the room slowly, a step and a stop, another step and stop, trying to sense if any spot felt different from any other—if there was one special place I should stand.

The room burst into light. Not the sort of light the wriggling creatures in the dirt provided. Not like the lights that brightened structures. More like Pradat's healing lights—bright and sharp as the mid-year sun. I couldn't see its source.

The ugly smell of Weast and its kind smoldered in my nose. The salty air dried my mouth. The dirt seemed suddenly alive, sending shocks along the soles of my feet. My bones ached. The air grew heavy, then heavier, pressing, driving me to my knees. I hunched my shoulders and ducked my chin—as if that could protect me. The heavy air was everywhere, pushing on my head, my back, my face, my stomach, my shins. I fell to the dirt on my side, closed my eyes, and rolled into a tight ball, my arms wrapped across my chest, each hand holding tight to the opposite shoulder.

The shocks that had started in my feet now ran along the length of my body. I twitched and turned, but couldn't escape it. The air pressed, turned cold, turned freezing. My teeth chattered uncontrollably. I tried to unroll but couldn't—as though my skin had melted to itself, impossible to pull apart. I pried my eyelids opened and looked down along my body, my pulse hammering in my head, terrified of what I might see.

Not melted flesh. Not melted, but freezing, frozen—even if I couldn't see it. I wanted to scream but the air pressed in too tight. My mouth wouldn't open. I slammed my eyes shut again, felt my face crunched into tiny folds and creases, my muscles cramped. The piercing light stabbed through my closed eyelids. It seemed to take days to make my arms unfold from across my chest and force my hands up to cover my eyes.

Had the lumani felt this? All those times, closed up in this chamber, had they been desperately cold and crushed this way? They'd lived through it. But I wasn't lumani. Not like they were. I was still doumana, with a body never meant for this.

The *Expectation of Returning*, the song we sing for doumanas reaching the end of their time, roared into my mind.

> *Sweet and merciful creator,*
> *too long have I been gone from you.*
> *My heart cries out in longing*
> *to join again with the soul.*

Jonton was outside the door. Larta. No one could save me.

> *Sweet and merciful creator,*
> *too long have I been gone from you.*

Freezing. Freezing. Shaking. Crushed.

I wanted it to end. Anything to make it stop.

The lights blinked out. I sensed it through my squeezed eyelids. The air pressure pushed a little less against my body. Slowly, slowly, the freezing lightened and became less painful though, even when it no longer hurt, I didn't open my eyes. I lay curled tight, breathing—grateful for the small joy of air sliding in and out of my nose and lungs.

Finally I forced my eyes open. The room looked no different from when I'd first stepped into it. It should have been wrecked, the walls crumbled, the floor full of cracks. I inched my hands to my scalp and rubbed gently with both hands.

I needed to sit up. I knew it, wanted it, but couldn't. Not yet. I lay a while longer, the dirt beneath me cool now, as comfortable and pleasant as lying in the fields with my sisters back at Lunge. I wouldn't look at my left wrist. The dots could be the same, still thirty-five.

That could mean nothing good had happened in this room. It could mean that the change took time. It could mean—

Birds that weren't birds chirped, twittered, and squawked somewhere around me. I levered up on one elbow and looked around, cocking my head different ways, trying to figure out where the sound had come from. The birds yammered again—below me, above me, from the walls.

A soft voice, like the barest breeze, sounded not in my earholes but inside my head—like think-talking, but different. Not like hearing so much as *knowing* the words already the moment they sounded.

Khe, the voice said, *I have given you back your years. Look now. Look and see the truth of this.*

I sat up slowly, half afraid to look, half afraid I was making up voices to say what I wanted to hear. I scratched the side of my neck with my right hand— buying time. Slowly I turned my left arm over and looked at my wrist. The dots were still there, a field of blue stars on red skin.

Not thirty-five.

I held my breath and started to count. When I was done, I counted them again. The number was the same both times: thirteen. Exactly the number there should be.

I sat a long time staring, delight singing in my blood, a grin as big as the wilderness stretched across my face.

Khe, the voice said, *your rightful years are my gift to you, a gift I have been waiting and hoping to give.*

My heartbeat sped. I glanced around the dirt room, wondering where the voice came from, if it were real or only something I imagined. Of course it was real—it was the same voice that had guided me through the cavern and brought me here.

Where are you? I thought-talked. *Can I see you? Can you be seen?*

I am here, the voice said—and the sound came from everywhere.

I watched as all the little luminous creatures that had lit the walls began moving down toward the bottom of the wall. When they reached the bottom, they crawled under the dirt floor toward me. Was it the creatures that'd brought me here, given me back my life? They wriggled toward me, then began to turn, forming themselves into a glowing circle around me.

Can you see clearly now? the voice asked.

Yes, I sent back. It wasn't the little creatures at all; it was the dirt, the planet itself, that fed me, that had given me physical energy. And now, its ultimate gift: my rightful years.

How can I thank you? I thought. *Can I offer you help? The shivering—I heard you sob.*

The ground rolled gently beneath me.

The machine, the planet sent, *brings me pain. I would be grateful if you destroyed it.*

The machine that made our world perfect. That brought the right weather for my sisters—and brothers—to thrive. Without the machine, what would happen to us?

What did I owe the planet that had given me back my life?

How could I choose between them?

I don't know how to destroy the machine, I thought, and

hoped that would spare me from having to decide.

I will help you when the time comes, the voice said. *I will give you the strength.*

I slowly pulled myself to my feet. I gazed at the solid door set into the dirt.

Can you open the door? I sent.

I'm sorry. No. I cannot do that without harming you.

A finger of fear raced up my chest. I didn't know how to open it from this side; didn't know if it *could* be opened from this side. But Jonton could open the door. And Larta had seen how she'd done it.

"Larta." My voice was little more than a rusty whisper.

No answer came.

"Larta!" I screamed, frightening myself with the force of the sound.

The door clicked and slid open. Larta and Jonton stood staring at me, the question in both their minds clear on their faces.

I walked toward them, holding my left arm up, forearm turned their way, laughter rising in me, until it burst out and rang like chimes against the dirt walls.

Jonton's eyes grew wide. She shoved me aside and ran into the room. The door shut hard behind her. I stared after her. The room, the confluence of energy, had extended the lumani's lives, and now mine. I supposed Jonton would get what she sought there as well.

Larta rested an arm over my shoulder, her neck brightly lit crimson. "Now we have to wait for Jonton."

I nodded. I'd had no sense of time in the room, no way to figure how long we would be waiting.

The voice whispered inside my head. *Go now. I will guide you. Jonton will not be back.*

I felt as though all the air had been sucked from the cavern in a great rushing plume. I couldn't make myself move. Jonton had done evil things, Returned four doumanas, an act I couldn't comprehend, but she deserved her life—and shunning—for a very long time. To be Returned herself would almost be a gift, a smaller pain than shunning would bring. But the planet had no use for the way doumanas thought. It had its own ways, its own punishments.

"Jonton won't be coming with us," I told Larta. "Likely she won't be coming back at all."

Larta gaped at me. Her neck showed the gray-red of shock and the soft-gray of sorrow, but she closed her mouth, nodded once, and we turned away.

And here was one more change made in us—that we would walk away and leave a doumana, any doumana, in jeopardy

In the last step of light before we re-entered the dark, tight passageway, I sneaked another look at the inside of my left arm. It felt wrong to be happy when Jonton faced misery, but I was happy. My rightful years were mine again.

I led the way back, the planet whispering directions in my ear, taking a different, more direct route than the way we'd come. Energy poured through me. Once we were beyond the tight passage I walked so fast Larta huffed from trying to keep up. I didn't slow until we came to the cavern beneath the machine room.

Larta looked up at the dirt roof above our heads. "Now what?"

I waited for help or instructions, but the voice was silent.

"I don't know," I said.

"Coming all this way just to find ourselves stuck," Larta said, running her hands over the walls, looking for a divot like the one Jonton had used to open the door at the heart.

"There's a way out," I said. "Jonton would have used it." My mind was spinning. Jonton had known the secret. She'd come and gone from the caverns enough times to know them well. Whatever the secret was, I couldn't see it.

I stood a moment, staring at the machine, wondering if it somehow controlled the way in and out. But Larta was likely more on track. Every door I'd seen in the Research Center had an eye or something that made it work. I slowly ran fingers that still ached from the heart room over the dirt wall, afraid I'd miss the spot.

Larta laughed once. "Found it."

I spun around to face her.

"Ready?" she asked

A sudden fizz of nerves flashed through me, but I nodded.

The flash was lightning-bright. I threw my hands up to cover my squeezed eyelids. An icy breeze blew past my legs. Then darkness.

I opened my eyes slowly, cautiously. We were back in the machine room. The weather machine was quiet now. No water fell into its full-to-the-top cache. The Returned guardians still lay where they had fallen. My neck burned. Larta's glowed bright with the soft-gray of sorrow and the black-red of rage.

The bird noise sounded low in my earholes.

It must be destroyed, Khe. You must help me.

The weather machine. The source of the planet's suffering.

How?

One last pain, the planet said. *One last shake. You must loose the water and let it pour down. Tell your sisters to leave this place if they wish to live.*

-=o=-

Larta had gone to Justice House, leaving me in the machine room after I'd told her what needed to be done. I couldn't look at the fallen guardians. I stood, staring at the machine—the face, metal the color of shadows, the only-for-show dials and levers—and wondered if it had consciousness. And if it did, was it happy or miserable at the use that had been made of it? And if it did, did I have the right to help in its destruction? The destruction, too, if I read the planet rightly, of the structure that housed it, with a consciousness of its own.

I was glad when Larta returned with several guardians, enough to do the two jobs needed now. Every guardian stood, stunned at the sight of their fallen sisters, every neck showing the dark-purple of grief and the brown-black of anger. They'd brought rolling cots. Each Returned guardian was tenderly placed on one and taken away. Back to Justice House, I presumed, but didn't know for sure.

The remaining guardians fanned out through the research center, herding the few doumanas still in the structure out.

Larta took hold of the elbow of the last guardian, and said, "I have a different assignment for you. Find Nez. Tell her we'll be sending out word about the council and inviting the representatives to come. Nez will represent Chimbalay and be the Speaker. She needs to prepare her words well. Khe and I will meet her outside Presentation House."

The guardian nodded, and then only Larta and I were left in the room.

"You're going to destroy the machine and the structure?" she asked.

Not me—the planet, I wanted to say, but even Larta, who knew that there were more things in our world than most doumanas were aware of, might find it hard to understand who spoke to me inside my head. I nodded.

"It's a bit like the Energy Center all over again," she said. "Here we are, destroying something needed by the doumanas of Chimbalay."

My neck went hot. I'd thought about that as well. "It's not the same. There's another research center in Chimbalay, a place for sick or hurt doumanas to find help," I said. "If no *research* goes on for a while, that might be a good thing."

Larta laughed once, quietly. "You're right about that. But what about the machine? We'll go back to inconsistent weather. To lean years. To suffering. You're the one who said it shouldn't be destroyed."

"I know," I said. "Things have changed. I'll try to explain it later, when we have some time. For now—"

Larta cut me off. "Do whatever needs to be done.

I'll stand by your side."

I reached out and stroked her neck in gratitude just as the text box strapped on her forearm vibrated, the movement so small it would be easy not to see, but she would feel it.

"We're the only ones left in the research center," she said. "The structures on either side and across the avenue have been emptied as well."

I drew in a deep breath and let it out slowly. Then I began the feathery words and hand movements that would start the machine working. I knew how to make the water in the catch-tube dump down deep into the world. How to make it happen fast or slowly. I made the motion for fast, and watched out of the side of my eye as water rushed from the tube until it was empty.

I felt a tiny shiver roll under my feet and then stop.

"Larta, it's time to go."

-=o=-

We stood across the wide avenue from the research center, our backs up against the three-level dwelling where the doumanas in charge of recreation lived—the structure empty now, the guardians having sent them to an outer ring for safety.

When the shivering began, I set my feet wide apart, bent my knees, and braced to ride it out. Larta touched my shoulder once, gave a little shrug, and set her legs the same way. We waited together for whatever was to come.

The shiver built, the planet grumbling beneath us, the ground buckling and rolling. I grabbed hold of a branch from one of the thick-trunked trees that flanked either side of the dwelling. The limb shook in my hands, the rough bark scraping my palms. Larta seized a different branch, but held on just as hard. The tree seemed to jump as the ground swelled under it, rising up. I felt myself rise too, my balance failing. I held tight as we slammed back down, and the ground began to sway violently from side to side. The research center shook like a reed in a windstorm. Tiles fell from the roof, crashing against the stone streets and breaking into tiny pieces. The air stank of ozone.

A roar tore the air. The ground shook back and forth beneath our feet. A jagged crack began crawling up the face of the structure. The crack widened, the wall splitting open like decaying fruit. The creak and screech as the skin of the structure broke apart rang loud in our earholes. I imagined other cracks on other walls we couldn't see from where we stood.

The research center groaned, and I listened, wondering if it were aware of the cracks splitting its sides, hoping it wasn't. Chunks of plaster, large and small, fell into the street. The planet gave a mighty twist and the research center fell, the structure folding in on itself, sinking into the hole that had been the machine room.

The shiver ended. A strange and total silence settled over Chimbalay.

TWENTY ONE

"Jonton told me her secret," Larta said as we walked toward Presentation House. The rubble of Research Center Three lay behind us. Already doumanas had arrived with tools and vehicles and were clearing the remains away. The shock of what we'd seen was fading.

"I asked," Larta said, "and Jonton was so proud of herself she couldn't keep from telling me how she knew what was said all over Chimbalay."

I had been thinking of Nez, wondering if I should tell her what I'd learned in the room of floating faces. I pulled my attention to Larta. "How did she do it?"

"Jonton told me the lumani wanted to 'study doumanas in their natural state'. They wanted to know what we did when we were alone with our sisters. She said that as fascinated as the lumani were with us, they didn't like us much. They didn't want to be near us physically if they didn't have to be."

That didn't surprise me. Weast had seemed interested but resigned during the time we spent together.

"The lumani," Larta said, "figured out a way to hear through clearstone. The way Jonton described it was that clearstone held the instant memory of everything said in front of it. The lumani learned to extract the memory. They showed her how it worked. Once the lumani were gone, she took it over for herself."

"So any room with a window was open to Jonton's listening," I said.

Larta nodded. "We kler doumanas love our windows. Every structure has as many as we can fit in."

I gave my admiration grudgingly, but it was an amazing thing the lumani had done—to make clearstone repeat back anything it heard.

We turned onto Bright Blue Circle—the street named for the color of excitement—and walked a while without talking, each with her own thoughts.

"Do you want to know my secret?" I asked Larta, unsure why it felt important to say it out loud at this moment, but knowing that it was. Larta seemed the perfect person to tell. Not Nez. Not Azlii. I supposed it was because though Larta was a sister, I would leave her here in Chimbalay when Kelroosh left, and that made her safer to tell, somehow.

"You have secrets?" She sent me a grin.

"Since that night," I said, "the night we destroyed the lumani, I've lived in fear of what I was becoming— would become—this creature that was not doumana and not lumani—something in between. Or worse—I would become all lumani."

Larta tilted her head and looked at me. "But you're not afraid any more. Not now. That's good."

"I don't understand why," I said, and hesitated to go on. A doumana should have her reasons clear and ready if she decides to make a confession. I was unprepared. "Maybe I'm resigned. Maybe I'm curious to see how I'll wind up." I thought it over. "I have time now. Before, everything was crashing down. I was changing, Commemoration Day was coming." I glanced at my wrist and the thirteen blue dots there. "Now, it's more like being a hatchling on Emergence Day—nervous, leaving one state behind, moving to another, but excited too. Whatever I am to be, I'll do my best with it."

Larta sniffed. "Our whole world is changing." She sent me a smile. "Whatever you become, whoever, I'm pleased to call you sister. You'll always have a welcome in Chimbalay so long as I am here."

We'd arrived at Presentation House. Nez was waiting by the wide steps. Her neck was wreathed in the orange-red of anticipation and the black-blue of determination. She wanted to do this for her sisters, for all the soumyo. My neck warmed and I wished Nez could see the color of my pride in her.

We started up the steps, climbing to a new life, a new world.

-=o=-

The night was warm, the sky clear. I sat alone in the garden behind Justice House, on the ground near the same tree where I'd met with Pradat. My cloak lay loose over my shoulders. My bare feet dug a finger's length into the loose soil.

Birds yammered nearby. No, not nearby—in my earholes, in my mind.

Are you there, Khe? the planet sent.

I wriggled my toes deeper into the soil. *I'm here. And I have questions for you.*

The soil around my feet loosened—the planet giving me welcome.

Do you have a name? I asked.

I do, but it's long and likely hard for you to say. Ah-sen-the is the start of it, and you may call me that.

"*Ah-sen-the,*" I said aloud, liking the feel of the word in my mouth and in my mind.

I scraped at the dirt with the ball of my foot, until the hole was ankle deep. The soil was warm and comforting on my skin. *Why did you save me?*

Birds chattered in my head again, but a different tone now, lower.

Jonton was right about some things, Khe. You are changed. But she was wrong to say you were becoming lumani. You may put that fear aside. You are nothing but doumana.

No, I thought. *I am changed. I see and hear better than my sisters are able to. I see emotion colors not just on a doumana's neck, but swirling throughout her body, the way the lumani saw.*

The bird chatter sounded again, and then, *You are no part lumani, Khe. You are merely the future—what all soumyo could be, will be. Not just improved vision and hearing, not just the ability to see another's true emotions, not even to go long periods without food or sleep, but to live in better harmony with your sisters and brothers, the plants and beasts, the structures— and with me.*

My breath caught in my throat. To not be lumani— to be what?

How could that happen? I sent.

The sound like a single raindrop beating over and over against wood rang in my head. I looked up quickly, expecting to see rain, but the sky was clear. The voice echoed inside my earholes.

Pradat started it with the procedure that let you first feel Resonance. The lumani made you more of what you already were.

You are the most a soumyo can be, but you are only soumyo, nothing else.

I rubbed my fingers lightly on the dirt. I wanted to believe all that the planet said. Wanted to, but—

If I am still only soumyo, why don't my emotion spots light?

They are no longer needed, not when you can see much deeper into your sisters' hearts.

My sisters don't see what I see, I sent. *They can't know what I feel. I think it bothers them.*

The silence that set in went on so long I thought the conversation was ended—the planet had finished talking to me and turned to other concerns.

I am sorry, Khe, the voice came finally. *It is never easy to be the first.*

I blew out a breath. That was true enough.

Thank you, though, I thought. *For caring for us. For giving me back my life.*

The low chittering of all the birds in the world rang in my mind.

It was selfish of me to save you. The corentans are close to harmony with me, but they don't know me the way you do. They don't hear me. They don't feel my heartbeat. The weather-prophets heard me, but couldn't believe it was their planet whispering softly to them about what was to come. They made up the idea of tasting the weather in explanation. I have been alone and lonely for a very long time. I need a sister, Khe. A unitmate. You could be that for me.

I slipped my fingers under the dirt. *I would be honored.*

A thought itched in my mind. *Why do you call saving me selfish?*

Because I so wanted you for a sister, I saved you while knowing that not all that has changed in you will be pleasant. I have given you back your life, but I may also have brought you grief.

May have brought?

No future is certain, Khe. I hope yours is only bright. Now you should rest.

Rest. I wanted that. Needed it.

The soil beneath me loosened and shifted, making a soft, curved impression to lie in. Stars shone through the tree leaves, so many that they could never be counted.

This is what I had learned: just because a thing is done, it doesn't mean all things are finished. Corentas would be arriving soon with the soumyo—doumana and male—who would make up the new council. Now that the rain had stopped, farming communes would begin planting. Commune leaders everywhere would have to begin making their own decisions. Some would be wise and some not. Commemoration Day would come and I would rise the morning after with more years to live.

I closed my eyes and, for the first time since the lumani, slept deep and long.

Dear Reader,

When I finished writing *Khe*, I thought I'd told her story and it was done. I followed *Khe* with *Shadowline Drift*, a completely different sort of tale, set on Earth, with (mostly) human characters. But Khe kept nagging at me, whispering in my ear that there was more, that things had happened after that final scene. I was curious—what had happened after? Tell me, I said to Khe. This book is the result.

As always, the writer only does half the job of creating a story. The other half is done by you, the reader, and I thank you for making this story live. If you would be so kind as to leave a short review on Amazon and/or Goodreads, I would appreciate it.

There are more stories to come. Next up is a tale of life on Khe's world before the lumani. If you'd like to receive the occasional email with new release information, please sign up for my mailing list here: http://eepurl.com/08229.

Thank you.

Alexes Razevich

Acknowledgments

Many thanks to Chip Downs, Dan McNeil, Don Machen, Meg Xuemei, Randy Jackson, Richard Casey, Robin Mattocks, Sue Marschner, and Wendy Scott—with special thanks to Jay Howard and Christina Frey, the best editors a writer could hope for—for their friendship and help in shaping Khe and her world.

Much love to Chris, Larkin, and Colin Razevich, who I adore beyond anything words can convey.

Cover art by Tony Honkawa, Tony Honkawa Design

About the Author

Alexes Razevich was born in New York and grew up in Orange County, California. She attended California State University San Francisco where she earned a degree in Creative Writing. After a successful career on the fringe of the electronics industry, including stints as Director of Marketing for a major trade show management company and as an editor for Electronic Engineering Times, she returned to her first love—fiction. She lives in Southern California with her husband. When she isn't writing, she can usually be found playing hockey or traveling somewhere she hasn't been before.

Alexes is always happy to hear from readers and welcomes new friends on Facebook and Twitter.

Email: LxsRaz@yahoo.com

Twitter: https://twitter.com/lxsraz

Facebook:
https://www.facebook.com/AlexesRazevichAuthor

New Release Mailing List: http://eepurl.com/08229

Website: http://www.alexesrazevich.com/

Also by Alexes Razevich

Khe (The Ahsenthe Cycle, Book 1)

Gama and Hest (The Ahsenthe Cycle, a companion story)

Shadowline Drift: A Metaphysical Thriller

GAMA AND HEST Sample

ONE

Outside, the air grumbled and growled. Hest shot Gama a quick look, his eyebrow ridges hiked up, making small dark furrows on his forehead. Gama shrugged and continued the chant. The old ones said it never rained on Emergence Day, and it hadn't—not in her lifetime or the lifetimes of the oldest among them. Still, the rumble plucked at her nerves.

Steam filled the windowless room, condensing on Gama's skin, making it glisten. Tiny transparent crystals formed in the heat, sliding down so infinitesimally slowly it was like the movement of stars. The steam was for the three hatchlings gathered there with the adults, to soften their outer skins and make shedding it easier. Once the skin was sloughed off, a new adult would stand before them, ready to join the community.

Hest's skin was lighter than Gama's. The droplets didn't stand out against his face as brightly as those on her skin. He lifted a hand—his smaller one, meant for liberating the egg during mating—and wiped away the moisture that wet his face.

It was a nice face, Hest's. Gama had liked it when she first saw it at their own Emergence, when their downy outer coatings had been stripped away and they had discovered themselves as adult soumyo. He had light orange-red skin that contrasted sharply with his black eyes, a thin but attractive chest, and one hand small and delicate—the one he was now using to wipe his face now—and the other sturdy, with a fine digger claw for routing out a nest at mating time. They were about the same height, but her skin was a darker and clearer red, her eyes yellow, and her female hands a perfect if opposite match.

Someone put more wood on the fire below two large cauldrons filled with water, aromatic leaves, barks, and roots. Gama heard the crack and sizzle of the new wood being fed to the flames. Scents sweet, woody, and savory filled the air. Standing at the back of the large room, she couldn't see through her kin to know who had done it, though her guess would have been Prill, Reln's apprentice.

Hest gently elbowed her side and mouthed the word, *male*. Gama shook her head. They'd played this game last year, too—predicting what gender each hatchling would be when it emerged. He was terrible at it, guessing male nearly every time—hoping for more of his own kind, she supposed. She was better at the game, and felt sure this one would be female. It pleased her to think she'd soon have a new sister.

When she was right, Hest slumped—exaggerated for effect, as usual—against the wall: plaster over stone and wood, the plaster mixed with pulverized green rocks to give it a bright color. He sent a thought her way, the thought-grains traveling silently across the short distance through the moist air: *You cheat, Gama.* Anyone looking at them would see the thought-grains moving, but by convention anyone who didn't receive the thought would ignore what they'd seen and not speculate on what was said.

She leaned next to him on the wall. It was impossible to cheat—no one could know a hatchling's gender in advance, though there were those who claimed to recognize the tiny signs of difference. Gama was wondering what those telltale signs might be when the world outside exploded.

A tremendous bang shook the room, louder than in the lightning storms last year that had lit the skies for days and brought thunder that made her ear holes ring. The wall they leaned against quivered, fear running through the structure the same as it ran through her.

"Out!" Reln, their guide, shouted and the structure threw open the door. Gama lunged toward the three new adults, their hatchling-down still lying at their feet, anxiety bright on their emotion spots. Before she covered four steps, Prill had reached the new adults and was leading them toward the door. Reln hastily put out the fires beneath the large cauldrons, smothering them with sand from the buckets kept full for that purpose. Hest grabbed Gama's hand, his digger claw a hard and comforting presence in her palm. She closed her fingers around it, holding tight.

Outside, everything looked the same—structures, dwellings, the commons, and the high wall around them, the parts of Reev she could see from where she stood. Nothing had collapsed or exploded. The sky was blue and cloudless. The heat on her emotion spots shifted as they changed from the blue-red of anxiety to the orange-yellow of confusion. The same colors showed on Hest's neck and on the throats of their sisters and brothers. Usually a harmony of feelings among her kin was a soothing sight. Now it bothered her, like having a stone in her foot casing but finding nothing there when she shook it out.

Hest nudged her and pointed up, out beyond Wall, above where the orchards they'd been harvesting stood. "Do you see that?"

She strained her eyes but saw only treetops and sky.

Above the trees, Hest thought-talked. *A sort of shimmer?*

Gama shaded her eyes with her hand and looked hard where he'd pointed, but didn't see anything unusual. Hest's lips pushed together in a line.

It was there, he sent.

She glanced at her sisters and brothers milling around them. They were nervous, disturbed, but none paid any attention to the sky. *It must have gone.*

Hest looked away, as though he couldn't bear it if she doubted him.

-=o=-

The second bang came in the night. Females and males poured from their dwellings, some hastily tying on hip wraps or throwing on cloaks, but most running without dressing, too panicked to even pull on foot casings to protect their feet.

Gama and Hest ran outside together, Home sending behind them, *What's happening? What's happening?* Gama shook her head, though she never knew how much structures could read gestures.

Their brothers and sisters filled the commons, everyone as confused as they were, some talking to the kin next to them, but most standing open-mouthed, glancing wildly in every direction, their necks aflame in the gray-red of shock or the muddy-brown of fear.

Another huge boom cut the air. Hest grabbed Gama's arm with his soft hand and pointed into the night sky with the other. Above them, off to the left, the air shimmered like sunlight on still water. Gama's heart beat fast. The frightened structures called to each other, all talking at once in their own speech that sounded like a long blow of wind. She leaned close to Hest, for the comfort of his skin.

"Look!" a sister called, her eyes on the sky.

A disk-shaped swath of stars went out—not one by one, but all at once, as though the sky had swallowed them whole. *We should go. We should go*, the structures sent in words Gama could understand. Wall flapped its five wooden gates open and shut, open and shut, as if desperate to get Reln's attention, since only he could make the decision for the corenta to move.

Gama grabbed Hest's hand and pulled him with her as she ran through the crowd toward their guide, ducking around their sisters and brothers. Reln stood transfixed, his head tilted back, his mouth hanging open. Gama grabbed his shoulders and shook them.

"You see that?" Reln stared hard at the sky.

Above their heads, burning blue flames filled a starless circle in the night sky. Gama stared as the circle grew, the licking flames filling in where stars had been. She stared so long and hard her eyes watered. She tightened her hold on Hest's hand.

Another boom rang out.

Behind it, low and deep—a hum.

And then the flames were gone, flicked out like covering a candle, the black circle of sky once again filled with stars.

Reln shut his mouth and dropped his chin, his gaze moving from face to face. Everyone waited for him to speak.

"Return to your dwellings," he said, raising his voice to be heard. "It's over now."

They turned slowly, the two hundred and fourteen sisters and brothers of Reev corenta, some confused, some frightened—everyone grabbing onto Reln's words and the calm, sure way he'd said them, as if he had a secret knowledge and they could trust those words completely.

Gama let loose of Hest and rubbed her hands over her thighs. It didn't feel over to her. It felt dangerous.